The Witch in Room 6

Edith Battles

The Witch in Room 6

1 8  1 7

HARPER & ROW, PUBLISHERS

Cambridge, Philadelphia, San Francisco, Washington, London, Mexico City, São Paolo, Singapore, Sydney

NEW YORK

The Witch in Room 6
Copyright © 1987
by Cheryl Suzanne Battles and Sean Nicholas Battles
Printed in
the United States of America. For information address
Harper & Row Junior Books, 10 East 53rd Street,
New York, N.Y. 10022. Published simultaneously
in Canada by Fitzhenry & Whiteside Limited, Toronto.
Designed by Joyce Hopkins
1 2 3 4 5 6 7 8 9 10
First Edition

Library of Congress Cataloging-in-Publication Data
Battles, Edith.
    The witch in room 6.

    Summary: When apprentice witch Cheryl Suzanne Endor
joins Sean's fifth-grade class, amazing things begin
to happen and Sean learns to accept as a friend and
appreciate as an individual someone who is very
different from himself.
    [1. Witches—Fiction.   2. Schools—Fiction.
3. Friendship—Fiction.   4. Individuality—Fiction.]
I. Title.   II. Title: Witch in room six.
PZ7.B3246Wi 1987   [Fic]   86-45785
ISBN 0-06-020412-5
ISBN 0-06-020413-3 (lib. bdg.)

To Kathi and Ralph and the entire Torrance Unified School District for providing the raw material for this book—whether or not they ever intended it.

Contents

An Old Enemy and a New One

The second bell rang just after Sean raced from the sunshiny outside corridor through the door. Now, he thought, he could sneak to his seat before Miss Jellenich noticed. But Mike's clarinet case suddenly filled the aisle.

As Sean tripped, his armload of books squirted across Margie's table. He didn't have to look up from the floor to know that Miss Jellenich was tapping her foot, arms folded over her chalk-dusty blouse.

"Here, let me help," said Mike, the clarinet case now innocently tucked back beneath his table. "Are you okay?" With a great show of concern, Mike delicately dusted and stacked Sean's books. He even replaced the loose homework papers. "There, now. Good as new."

Sean mumbled, "Thank you," for Miss Jellenich's sake. Miss Jellenich smiled her approval at Mike.

She wouldn't have been so approving, Sean thought, if she had known that Mike was the only fifth-grade boy to get out of detention when they had been caught looking at Margie's father's magazine last Thursday noon.

Sean had to breathe deeply to control his anger.

The class rose for flag salute. Sean stayed up for the cafeteria lunch count. Today was chili beans and broccoli—not his favorites—but he'd forgotten to pack a sack this morning. (Everybody worked at Sean Wilkerson's house—his father at a new building construction site, his mother in her boutique, and his high school sister, Kelly, at The Slinkery where people on diets went for dessert. Sean packed his own lunch or ate cafeteria chili.)

It was math time, but a stirring at the door drew all their glances. Mr. Drake, the principal, stood in the doorway. With him was a tall woman whose gray hair was skewered with pins into a doughnut on top of her head. Her old-fashioned dress dragged to her ankles. She stood beside a girl with lank, black hair who looked around ten years old, Sean's age.

"Good morning, Miss Jellenich. Good morning, boys and girls. We have a new fifth grader for you today." Mr. Drake's voice sounded very cheerful, not a bit like his tone last Thursday in his office.

Sean had no use for girls except for his sister, Kelly, who was too grown-up to count. Still, he had noticed with a tug of interest that, after summer vacation, nearly all the girls had come back thicker and taller. Some were even a little lumpy. But this girl, in her bunchy, dust-colored dress, was narrow and scrawny.

She carried a gray enameled lunch pail straight out of an old-time TV show. And instead of checking out her new room the way new kids usually did, she stared right at Sean. He knew instantly that this girl spelled *trouble*!

2

"Oh, no," he thought. "Don't let her sit by me. Let Margie yak her ear off or let Joe share his junk heap, but don't let her sit by me."

The class revved up. No matter what any new kid looked like, everybody had to talk and show off. But Sean just looked away and sat as fat as he could.

"Boys and girls," Mr. Drake repeated, a bit louder. The noise settled. "Cheryl Suzanne Endor is here all the way from Massachusetts. I know you will make her welcome."

Sean counted to ten before he looked up. Mr. Drake and the gray-haired woman were leaving. From the back, the woman's angular shape reminded him of someone he had seen in his own neighborhood. But he couldn't have seen her before, not if she'd just moved here from Massachusetts.

"How do you do, Cheryl Suzanne?" Miss Jellenich's voice was sugary, too. "Let's see. Where shall you sit?"

Sean watched her tick off the places. Margie? Margie kept begging for a seatmate, but she had worn out every one since kindergarten with her endless talking. Even Sean could tell that Margie wouldn't be able to rave about designer clothes or rock stars with Cheryl Suzanne Endor.

Miss Jellenich passed right over Margie and on to Joe. The space around Joe was like a toxic dump. Just now, he scrubbed pencil lead into a jagged design on his hard plastic tabletop. He used up two pencils a week polluting the inside and outside of his table. Before Miss Jellenich let him leave each afternoon, he spent cleanup time wearing down an eraser. Sean thought the tabletop al-

3

ways looked cleaner than Joe, whose hands were permanently gray, as if he wore graphite gloves.

"Cheryl Suzanne will sit by you, Sean," said Miss Jellenich brightly.

Sean slumped. Then he drew a deep breath. He reached over and slowly pulled out the three textbooks he had just stuffed into the borrowed half of his table. He crammed them inside on his own shelf. He did not turn or look up.

"Sean," said Miss Jellenich with gentle firmness, "will you show Cheryl Suzanne where to put her lunch? And will you find her the books she needs?"

"Yes, Miss Jellenich," he sighed.

Sean stood up and swept away the girl's enameled pail like a football in a handoff. He shoved it into an empty pigeonhole between the other bright plastic lunch boxes and pink paper sacks.

Still feeling mean and grumpy, he found the oldest fifth-grade math book in the stack. All the social studies books were new, so he took the one on top.

The health book was just right. It had eroded in Joe's desk until the day Rhonda needed a book because she'd left hers at home. Mike had helpfully told Miss Jellenich that Joe kept two health books. The smiling boy on the gray book cover had two teeth blacked out.

Sean returned to his desk and pushed the books across to Cheryl Suzanne. "Thank you, Sean," she said in a whispery voice.

He finally gave her a long look.

Why couldn't she wear the usual knit shirt and pants

the other girls liked instead of that jettisoned space suit? His glance locked with hers. Her gray-green eyes flashed him a measuring look, as if she was expecting something from him. But what?

He looked away and sat sideways so his back was all she could see. He could hear her putting away her books.

A folded pink note banked off Sean's shirt and landed in front of him. From Margie, of course. When she didn't jabber, she scribbled. His hand covered it quickly and moved it to his pocket to yawn over later.

"Boys and girls, please turn to page thirty-eight in your math books."

Sean reached into his desk for the math book he had just shoved there. He pulled it out. Yesterday's homework paper was sticking between the pages where Mike had placed it.

But look! The cover of the book wasn't new and shiny, as it had been minutes ago. It was old and pencil-marked, like the book he had just picked for Cheryl Suzanne!

From the corner of his eye, Sean looked around as she, too, took a math book from her shelf.

His book!

Yes, it must be his book. She held it in front of her and raised her eyes. "What page did she say?" whispered Cheryl Suzanne sweetly.

How had she had time to switch the books? Maybe he shouldn't have turned his back.

Sean swallowed.

"Sean, please pay attention," said Miss Jellenich. Sean sat up straight. Behind him, Mike made a yukking noise.

"Without that silly noise, please," said Miss Jellenich, still looking at Sean.

Sean clamped his mouth even tighter shut. First this girl, and now Mike!

Math went all right. When Miss Jellenich asked the new girl to multiply sixty-five times ninety-two, she worked the problem the very first time, almost as fast as Mike could when he used the tiny calculator he bragged about hiding in his math book.

When math time was over, Miss Jellenich asked them to close their books and listen. "Monday is the day of our field trip to the museum." Miss Jellenich taught both math and social studies, and the field trip was planned to study United States history and geography. "Mike's mother is coming along to help us." She smiled at Mike as if he had done something special by conning his mom into helping on a field trip. How could he even keep her from coming? Sean wondered. Mrs. Donlou sure had shown up fast last Thursday when most of the Room 6 boys were sweating out the noon hour in Mr. Drake's office for looking at the magazine Margie had told them was in the shrubbery behind the backstop.

"Mike will be in charge of one group and—let's see— Sean, you'll lead the other. Will you boys come forward and choose teams?"

Good. For once, Miss Jellenich gave Sean a choice about the people he'd sit near. And it was great not to be on Mike's team.

Sean liked Miss Jellenich. He liked her plumpness. He liked the way her dress and the tip of her nose at-

6

tracted chalk dust—sort of the opposite of Joe, who attracted grime. But just because Sean plugged away and got his work done on time, even hard reading, Miss Jellenich used him. She had him do odd jobs. Oh, not the choice jobs like taking a note around the classrooms so he could miss social studies. Mike always leaped up for those. But Sean got the sticky, little-kid jobs like emptying the wastebasket just before the recess bell rang.

Feeling important but trying to look cool, he stood beside Mike at the front of the room. Most of the boys looked at him hopefully. No one ever said it out loud—after all, Mike's dad was coach of their Saturday football team—but the boys didn't like Mike much either. Some of the girls thought Mike was the greatest. Well, he could have all the girls.

Miss Jellenich was being extra generous. "You may choose first, Sean."

Sean looked past Cheryl Suzanne at red-haired Steve and long-armed Dino, his good friends, trying to decide which to name first.

"Quickly, please."

"I choose—*Cheryl Suzanne?*" said Sean, his voice rising in shock. How had *that* come out of his mouth? He shook his head to clear it.

A slow titter rose across the room and swelled to a wave of laughter. He'd never hear the end of it.

His eyes met Cheryl Suzanne's. Behind her smile was a look of triumph.

"Why, it's like she *made* me call her name!" Sean realized. "Somehow she made me choose her first."

His face was hot. He felt furious. Under the noise, Mike jibed at him. "Aw, you beat me to Miss Yardstick of Massachusetts. How will I ever get over it?"

Then Mike chose Steve, everybody's favorite. When Sean chose this time, he had no trouble saying Dino's name. But Dino seemed unhappy at being on the team of such a dumb leader.

Sean hardly heard himself name the rest of his group. Back at his seat, he listed them. At least he wasn't stuck with Margie. Just to have that new girl along was bad enough. But, since he'd picked her first, he had to sit beside her on the bus! Both ways, he would have to sit next to Cheryl Suzanne.

"Recess time, children," said Miss Jellenich, just as if the kids weren't already shoving back their chairs. Sean waited until everyone was outside the room before he rose. But it didn't help.

The boys were waiting at the doorway, grouped as if they were on TV. Mike was the dramatic conductor, leading them in a chant:

> "Shaw-yawn has a girr-ull fray-end,
> Shaw-yawn has a girr-ull fray-end,
> Shaw-yawn has a girr-ull fray-end,
> Kiss, kiss, kiss!"

Girlfriend, nothing. Enemy!

II

The Magical Pest

Sean pushed past the cluster of fifth graders. Looking neither right nor left, he stopped at the drinking fountain. In late September, Southern California was hot and dry, with a burning Santa Ana wind from off the desert. By now, most of the kids had drunk their fill.

He looked down thirstily at the stream of water he was sipping. It dropped lower. His mouth followed it down. Suddenly, it rose like a mushroom and splashed his face. Standing back, he shook his head, not really minding the cool spray.

There, drinking innocently in the spot beside him, was a girl with lank, black hair and a bright pink dress. *Pink?*

It was Cheryl Suzanne, all right, but where was that faded, dusty dress she had worn just before recess?

He blinked his eyes. No, the dress wasn't pink at all. It was some crazy effect of getting water in his eyes. She still wore the same no-color bunchiness she'd worn all morning.

Cheryl Suzanne appeared to notice him. "Hello, Sean."

"H'lo," he grumbled, and dashed around the corner to the boys' rest room. Let her try to get past *that* door!

Sean used a paper towel to dry his face and hair. As his hand brushed his pocket, Margie's note crackled. He pulled the note out to throw in the waste bin. Still, he might as well see what she was gabbling about *this* time. He unfolded and smoothed it out.

> Sean—come to my house after school
> today. My dad works late and my mom
> will be gone and I know how to
> turn on their X-rated TV.

Not on her life! Sean wadded the note again. Mr. Drake had called all the boys' parents last Thursday about looking at the centerfold. In fact, he had kept the magazine in a manila folder right on his desk in case they needed to see.

Sean's mother and father were not pleased. This was no time to be caught watching adult TV at Margie's house.

He pushed the door and stepped outside, remembering to check both directions to avoid Cheryl Suzanne.

There she was, standing hopefully at the edge of a cluster of girls. Margie was in the middle. She was whispering something, and the girls shrieked with laughter. The noise stopped as they followed Margie's glance to where Cheryl stood. In silence, they looked her over. Sean noticed again how bunchy and different her clothes were from the other girls' bright outfits. The girls turned

10

back to Margie and kept their voices low until Cheryl Suzanne walked slowly on.

Sean headed for the handball court. The blacktop paving felt warm through the soles of his shoes, but the wind blew cooler here. Maybe there was still time to get a turn before the bell ended recess.

Probably not. He was eleventh in line. Mike always managed to be first. In a T-shirt that said *Hawaii*, Mike showed off his biceps and his handball skill. He missed at last and lined up right behind Sean. "Doing jazzercize with the girls?" Mike asked sweetly, brushing his brown, designer-cut hair back into place.

In stony silence, Sean waited his turn. He knew he had hardly a minute before recess would end. Steve missed a low ball, and then it would be Sean's turn. But the ball bounced—zigzag, zigzag—until it hit a tetherball post and quite surprisingly rebounded onto the roof of the building.

Sean slapped his leg in exasperation. He wouldn't get a turn, and now nobody else would be able to play handball for the rest of the day. Only the custodian was allowed on the roof of the building.

"May I play?" asked a whispery voice.

It was Cheryl Suzanne.

"Take Sean and go jazzercise," said Mike.

"There's no ball now," Sean told Cheryl, more politely than he meant to be because Mike was so rude.

"If I get you a ball, may I play?"

Sean shrugged. He couldn't lose anything by agreeing. But hey! There she was, bouncing the ball! She bounced it to Sean. He looked it over. It was clearly marked *Room 6*, the identical ball that had landed high on the roof.

"Sneak," said Mike to Sean under his breath.

No one else seemed to notice that a lost ball had popped out of nowhere. Sean was puzzled, but, after all, it was *his* turn. He won on a single return, and then it was Cheryl Suzanne's try.

Trying to make each other miss, Cheryl and Sean hit the ball against the wall. They dipped in and hit it and ran out and ducked back. Neither seemed to stop the other. Then Cheryl missed in a dumb swoop. Too dumb.

Now Sean faced Mike. Sean hoped the bell would ring now. Mike was very good at handball. Sean glanced at Cheryl. "I think something is wrong with the bell," she said, as if she knew what he was thinking.

Sean surprised himself. He played a good game against Mike, diving low for the grounders and jumping high for the lofty rebounds. It felt great to play so well. To Sean's delight, Mike lost an easy low one. What a game! Then, like a row of dominoes, the other boys and girls went down to him, one by one.

Why didn't the bell ring? Recess went on and on. Now it was Cheryl Suzanne's turn again. He tapped the ball to her, getting a little spin on it. She returned it to the wall, and it came directly back to him. "I'll slam it," he decided, knowing that she'd miss. But, with his fist raised, he watched the ball drift like a feather just out of reach. He missed it completely.

Mike took his turn. In two plays, Cheryl had him out. At least Mike couldn't tease Sean about being beaten by a girl.

Cheryl Suzanne tilted her head. "Is this game a little macho for you, Mike? Maybe you'd better try jazzercise."

The bell rang.

At the classroom door, Miss Jellenich had a worried look. "Boys and girls, get your readers and hurry to your classes quickly. The clocks are mixed up, and recess was a half hour long."

A little smile played around Cheryl Suzanne's mouth.

Sean went on to his own reading level, but Cheryl had to stay with Miss Jellenich to be checked for placement. Sean knew without question that, no matter how she actually read—a high level like Mike or kind of lowish like Sean—Cheryl Suzanne was going to end up in his own section.

Anyway, he wouldn't have her near him at lunch. If you bought your lunch, you ate in the cafeteria; if you carried lunch, you sat in the covered patio.

But, at noon, Cheryl didn't get her enameled pail from the shelf. She just lined up behind him in the cafeteria group, jingling coins. He looked over at the shelf where he had placed the pail himself.

"What lunch box?" she whispered with wide eyes. She followed him all the way to the cafeteria lunchroom line.

Sean solved that. He stepped out of line to get a drink of water. He noisily pulled and restuck the plastic grip-

13

pers on his shoes three times. Being at the end of the line was better than being up in front next to Cheryl Suzanne.

"Hello, Sean," said a whispery voice.

He shuddered. How had she managed to get right behind him again?

The smell of broccoli was strong as they reached the door leading to the kitchen service counter. A student helper rang the register and took Sean's money. Chili beans, broccoli, and Cheryl Suzanne—what a lunch!

Behind the wide, steaming counter that separated her from the children, the perspiring cook had a stack of half-filled trays ready to add the hot food at the last minute. She whisked an empty kettle from the counter to the stove behind her and turned with a puzzled look. "Isn't that strange? I was sure I cooked another pot of beans! My count is all wrong today. Will you two eat hot dogs and fresh melon?"

His favorites! The cook served them piping hot frankfurters and beautiful slices of yellow melon. Sean took the tray happily just as the cook exclaimed, "Well, doesn't that beat all! Here's a full kettle of beans and a full pan of broccoli."

Sean and Cheryl Suzanne left the kitchen and carried their trays past the envious eyes of row on row of students to the fifth-grade table. With a spoonful of beans halfway to his mouth, Mike just stared.

Cheryl enjoyed her melon. "It's as nice as those I grow myself."

Sean gobbled fast and stepped out into the sunshine

before Cheryl Suzanne was through eating. To be sure she wouldn't follow, he took his usual escape route to the boys' room. "How's your girl?" asked Steve, drying his hands.

Sean groaned. Steve was supposed to be his buddy. "She's not my girl," he growled. "She's a pest. Besides, she's skinny." He knew he wasn't being quite fair.

"Thin is in," said Steve. Then he smiled wickedly. "Want to scare her? I swiped this from my kid brother's bake-a-monster kit." He pulled a plastic spider from his pocket. It was furry-looking, big, black, and wriggly.

The spider cost Sean a whole package of gum. Just before social studies, he managed to hide it in Cheryl's desk. He put it on the middle of her shelf. When she pulled out her book, it would fall into her lap.

Sean gave a secret sign to Steve. Steve had passed the word, and all eyes were watching as Cheryl Suzanne reached for her social studies textbook.

A wriggly fake tarantula fell on her dress.

"Thank you, Sean. That's a lovely gift," Cheryl whispered. "Oh."

Even Miss Jellenich looked up at the sound of disappointment.

"It's not alive at all. It's only plastic."

Sean just sat and breathed. That girl. *That girl.*

At cleanup time, Miss Jellenich gave Joe his usual crisp reminder to undo the day's artwork. Then she reminded them all about the field trip on Monday.

The thought was enough to spoil Sean's whole weekend.

15

III

At the Wilkerson House

Sean kicked his book bag all the way down the sidewalk to his house on Diablo Drive. His sister, Kelly, was already home from high school, so Sean wiped his feet on a mat printed *WILKERSONS* and went through the front entryway instead of using his key at the back.

He found Kelly in the kitchen cutting two slabs of thickly iced carrot cake. "Here," she said. "Help me stoke up on calories so I can face four hours at The Slinkery."

She pushed a plate at Sean. "Can you hang out on your own till Dad gets here?" Their mother was always busiest on Friday nights, the best time for boutique sales.

"Sure." Sean knew the rules: *Lock up and stay put.* "Do you have to leave right away?"

Kelly's hurrying fork paused as she caught his wistful look. "No real rush. Is Mr. Drake over his tizzy about 'adult' art?"

"Oh, sure. I don't think he was really mad—just wanted

to throw a scare into us about 'appropriate' behavior at school. I guess I'm really teed off at Mike Donlou."

Kelly giggled, almost choking on her cake. "You should have seen his mother at The Slinkery the other day. She ate three big servings of whipped air and got free refills on the tea. But she had a box of doughnuts along to eat with them. What's new with Mike?"

"Same old Mike. What's new is a skinny girl from Massachusetts named Cheryl Suzanne. She sits by me. Everybody thinks I like her. But I really hate her."

"Why?"

"Well, I think she likes *me*."

Kelly chewed her last bite thoughtfully. "Good solid logic there."

Sean's ill humor fell away as it always did around Kelly. "Remember," she often reminded him, "I was an only child until I asked for you. It may have been a dumb move, but at least I'm loyal."

She rose. "Gotta go now. I'm bigger than you, so you get to put the plates in the dishwasher. Have a good game tomorrow morning." Kelly liked to sleep in on Saturdays.

Sean locked the door after her. The next hour would be lonely. He carried the dishes to the sink and stacked them in the dishwasher the way his mother liked.

Sean thought his mother was pretty. When she smiled, she had crinkly little wrinkles around her eyes, and she smiled a lot. She was usually brown-haired, but once in a while she experimented with black or gold. Her shop

17

kept her very busy, so she tried to make time for Sean in little ways that counted and left unexpected reminders for him when she was away. This morning, on his bathroom mirror, she had taped an envelope and some penciled instructions:

> Please use these behind your ears or under your fingernails or on your forehead when you forget your haircut next week.

Inside the envelope were printed stickers:

**I LOOK LIKE THIS BECAUSE
I AM A HELPLESS, NEGLECTED CHILD
WHOSE MOTHER WORKS.**

Sean laughed and stuck the stickers in his pocket. He had scrubbed his ears until he was almost late for school.

The sun was low. Dad ought to be home soon. As long as Sean could remember, since back when he was three or so, his father had worn a curly beard. "I was born that way," Dad explained with a twinkle when Sean asked what his face looked like underneath.

Sean was too little at the time to argue the fact, but later he took it up with Kelly. Her eyes danced. "There's nothing there at all. It's just a black hole in space where planets get lost."

Sean went to his mother as a last resort. "I don't really know, myself. Do you suppose he's covering a weak chin?"

This past summer, Sean had finally been old enough to help his father at the construction site. He only worked two hours a day for pocket money, but he felt very grown

18

up. "Do I call you Will, like the other men do?" he had asked his dad.

" 'Mr. Wilkerson, sir,' will do," joshed Dad. Dad's crew liked their boss. So did Sean.

"What, no TV? No homework? No microwave dinner waiting for a hungry father?" Dad came in the back door as Sean sat looking at the sunset.

Sean hugged him and then ran to rummage in the freezer. He could forget about Mike Donlou, whose parents were always around to back him up. Busy as Dad was, Sean knew he came home early the nights Mom worked, just for him. Sean made the most of every minute until Dad kissed him good-night.

Although Sean's mother had come in late, she was up early on Saturday. She always made sure Sean ate a good breakfast—his favorite scrambled eggs and orange juice and a not-so-favorite bowl of fiber cereal she claimed was good for him.

While Sean ate, his mother jogged. Every morning, she set the circular trampoline in the middle of the kitchen floor. Then she jogged five hundred paces without going anywhere. Sometimes she danced and flung her arms. Sometimes she skipped rope. But she always stopped at five hundred and said, "Oh, blanket!"

This morning Sean asked, "Why do you always say 'blanket,' Mom?"

His mother wiped her forehead with a paper towel. "I'm saying 'blank it!' There are children present, so I can't substitute a stronger word for *blank*."

19

"I know one," said Sean helpfully as she hastily covered his mouth.

"There are adults present," she reminded him. Then she checked his ears and nails.

"I'm not a neglected child this morning," Sean said. "Thanks for the eggs, Mom."

"Kids!" said his mother, shaking her head. "They sure are worth it!"

They both rushed to get ready. Sean had a football game, and his mother had her usual big Saturday at the boutique. Her car headed downhill as he sprinted up to the park.

Most afternoons and every Saturday, the fifth-grade boys worked out at the park. Last spring, it had been league baseball. Sean had tried hard, but he was never quite good enough to play more than a few innings in any game. But now his muscles were strong from hammering all summer, and he hoped to do a better job this football season.

Every team member had had to sell raffle tickets to get uniforms and shoulder pads. Unfortunately, Sean had knocked on all the neighborhood doors where the other players had knocked already. Finally, to unload his last tickets, he had had to call his grandmother. She got five discounts on pizza and five chances to win a rock concert pass.

Once he had his uniform, Sean surprised himself at his running plays. Today, the first game of the year, he would start as right halfback for the Blue team in the town football league. Nearly every boy his age in the neighborhood played, too. They all had new uniforms and very little appetite for pizza.

The players were gathering on the green. Sean waved to Steve, who was covering his red hair with a helmet. Steve ran out to receive passes from Mike.

Mike.

As usual, Sean's stomach turned over. The real problem was that Mike's father was their coach.

IV

A Strange
Football Game

Sean really liked Coach Donlou. Coach was a big man who knew his football. At one time, he had played for UCLA. But it was too bad, Sean thought, that he had such a one-track mind about Mike.

Sean admitted to himself that Mike was a good player. Coach Donlou had sensible reasons for naming him team quarterback. There were other kids, like Steve, who played almost as well, but nobody on the Blues really measured up to Mike. Sean knew it was unsportsmanlike to beef.

But Mike wasn't always a good sport himself. He was just too clever to be found out. Sean was positive that Mike sometimes called bad plays deliberately. The other boys agreed. To spectators, it always looked as if the other player had flopped in spite of Mike's strategy. Mike himself usually managed to look great.

Today had become cool with a hint of October chill, but Sean was warm in his padded uniform. It was still early, so Sean took his time before joining his teammates. He slowed his pace and looked around the grass-covered field with its frame of wooden bleachers on either side where the parents and brothers and sisters sat. Not any Wilkersons were there, of course. Sean pushed aside a small wistful feeling.

"Hi, Sean!" yelled a fourth grader. The younger kids loved to watch the older guys play.

Near the other goalposts, the Green team practiced lateral passes. They were fifth graders, too, but in their uniforms some of them looked mighty big. Sean felt a thrill of half fun, half fear. Today *he* had to look good against that team.

There she sat, old bad luck herself, Cheryl Suzanne, on the far right end of the wooden stands. She sat alone, eating a frozen ice-cream bar. He could see her face brighten as he looked her way. "Hi, Sean!" she called, and her voice came clearly all that distance, until the other guys looked up and began to make silly noises.

"Hi, Sean, dearie," said Dino, wrapping his long arms about himself and making kissing sounds.

Mike had just pulled off his helmet as he came off the field. "Ho!" he said. "So your girlfriend has come to see the great star."

"Oh, great!" thought Sean. "Now Mike will have it in for me because he doesn't like Cheryl Suzanne. He's going to make me look as bad as he can."

"All right, men," said Coach Donlou, a tall, broad-chested man with frown lines about his eyes. He almost

23

never smiled. "Let's get some practice before the Greens take their turn. Mike, you and Sean set up those running plays."

The Greens went off the field, and the Blues lined in T formation facing each other, half on offense, half on defense.

Coach Donlou blew a whistle to start the scrimmage.

Mike received the snap from center and spun to fake a handoff to the fullback. Instead, as they had planned it at Thursday practice, he handed the ball to Sean. But there was one difference. He put a little extra thrust into the handoff and knocked the wind out of Sean as the ball hit his already churning stomach.

Sean swallowed and recovered, but the delay was enough to get the defensive men in position. They were a stone wall of power when he ran into them, and there was no time to run around end.

Sean was shaken and angry. They lined up again exactly at their earlier spot. This time, Mike received the ball from center and tossed a lateral to Sean. It was just the way they had planned it on Thursday. Almost.

The ball was low and to one side—not much, but enough. Sean fumbled. He slowed and picked the ball up with a quick scoop, but the defending players landed on him. Even though they were all his good buddies, they weighed as much as a load of cement. He was glad for his helmet and shoulder pads.

They lined up again with a three-yard loss. "Oleo fingers," Mike muttered backward to Sean.

Mike called two more plays. Each time, Sean was the

24

receiver and ran, but he had no choice. He had to go through the hardest spot in the defending lineup, just as Mike had called it. Sean had the wind knocked out of him in every play. He was panting and tired.

"Sit awhile, Sean," Mike's dad said, a worried frown on his face. "You'd better rest before the game. Get the kinks out and you'll be back in form."

Wearily, Sean pulled off his helmet and headed for the bench. He watched the rest of the practice and then he watched the Greens go through their paces. They looked mighty good. Would Mike take a chance on losing the game just to show up Sean?

"Move over," said a voice. That voice and drab, gray sweater could belong to only one person. Sean moved over before he could check himself. He felt so bad already, he guessed he couldn't feel any worse. "Girls don't belong on the bench," he growled.

"Equal opportunity," said Cheryl Suzanne, sitting down. Was that another ice-cream bar? It never seemed to get any smaller. "This is fun to watch," she said. "I like the way you make all the players fall on top of you each time."

"Look," said Sean. "School I can stand. I *have* to sit next to you and listen to dumb talk. But not on Saturday. Go away."

"Oh," said Cheryl Suzanne. "You mean you aren't supposed to be on the bottom of the pile?"

"No, and you're not supposed to be here. Scatter."

"Oh, I thought it was fun to make them work so hard. Some of them didn't even get a chance to climb on top."

25

She sounded a little sorry. "Well, what *is* the reason for this game?"

Didn't she watch TV? Was Massachusetts located on Mars? "Look. Would you believe that I'm supposed to get my hands on the ball and then carry it past all the other guys until I get it across the goal line? I'm not supposed to lose it or get knocked flat."

"Are you the only one who's supposed to take care of the ball?"

"There are eleven guys on the other team and at least ten guys on mine who wish they had their hands on it instead."

"Oh, I see."

She sat quietly. He almost forgot her as he watched the Greens work out. They were fast! Then, "Say, Sean. I noticed that Mike has the ball a lot. Does he have to do that for the team to win?"

"He's quarterback," Sean said shortly. "He does want the team to win. We all do. But it doesn't mean other guys like to be left out."

"Would it be more fun if *you* got the ball?"

"Keech," grunted Sean, shaking his head. "If I want the team to win, I have to admit that Mike is the best player we have. He may be mean, but he's got speed and style. Maybe I'm kinda jealous."

"Speed and style," mused Cheryl. "Is that all it takes? Well, why don't *you* use speed and style? I know you can. You're as good as Mike."

"Huh?" Was this Cheryl Suzanne Endor talking?

Coach Donlou neared the bench as the Greens ran

from the field. Cheryl slipped away, but not before Mike saw her. He glanced to be sure his dad was busy with a referee, then shouted, "Peril, peril! Look out for Cheryl!"

With a sunshiny smile, Cheryl looked around and began to stick out her tongue—but took another lick of the ice-cream bar and headed back to the stands.

The game started, and the Greens chose to receive. Sean had been right about them. They were faster and bigger. At the end of the third down, they swept ahead six to zero. They converted with a high, soaring kick, and the score was seven to zero.

Back at the center, it was the Blues' turn to receive the ball. Steve caught the kick and returned it to the forty-yard line before he was stopped.

On down one, Mike tried the play he had first used with Sean—a fake handoff to the fullback and then a real handoff to the left halfback, Steve. But this time, Mike played it straight. Steve took the ball lightly and ran, but he gained only a little over a yard before the Green linemen blocked him solidly.

At lineup again, Mike took the ball from center, broke the T formation to lateral a pass to Steve, and raced ahead, hoping to receive a forward pass right back. But, to Steve's despair, the ball spilled out of his grasp and landed, luckily, in Sean's outstretched hands. Sean ran a few zigzags until the Greens pushed him down.

It was the third down, and the Blues had lost yardage on the earlier plays. Sean knew that Mike had to play it right. Steve was unstrung. Would Mike deliver the ball to Sean this time and give him a real chance?

A runner came in to substitute for one of the Blue linemen, and the players huddled to hear his message. Mike had no choice now. His dad had said to give Sean the ball.

Time-out over, they lined up. Mike called the signals, and the center handed the ball through his legs to Mike's waiting hands.

The ball slipped.

The easiest play in football is to receive the ball from center. The center sets it up. The ball rests on the ground pointing to the goals. The center hears the signal and delivers the ball with a slap right into the quarterback's right hand. All the quarterback has to do is take it.

But Mike Donlou missed.

The ball bounced and leaped crazily. Everyone on both teams was scrabbling for it, but it homed right to Sean's astonished grasp.

The surprised Greens stood lead-footed as Sean caught the ball on the run. He sped past them and into a clear field, running easily all the way to the goal line while they trailed, stunned, behind him.

The parents and the third and fourth graders all cheered. Sean's eyes swept the stands to see Cheryl wave her ice-cream bar at him.

Mike elected to convert. The kick spun sideways. The crowd groaned. Suddenly, the ball was caught by a gust of wind and came down to Sean's waiting arms. It was incredible. His gasp of astonishment was drowned out by the roar of the crowd, and Sean found himself running again to get across the goal line.

What a recovery!

Sean had earned two points instead of the one that Mike had tried for.

At halftime, the score was ten to eight in favor of the Greens. They hadn't been able to make another touchdown, but they'd kicked a field goal.

Sean took a sip of water as he gathered with the other players at the bench. "You made a couple of good recoveries there," Coach Donlou said. "I wonder what came over Mike."

Mike was last to join the group, not meeting anyone's eyes as he edged in surlily. His father scowled at him once or twice, but reviewed the plays in a quiet voice, even more controlled than usual. He didn't quite succeed in hiding his puzzlement.

Then Coach Donlou talked strategy and suggested which plays might go best in the second half. "Do some thinking on it, men. Maybe you'll come up with something we never tried in practice. Oddest game I've ever coached."

They broke up and spread along the benches. Steve walked with Coach Donlou, and Sean heard him say, "This game is so crazy, it's turning out like my baby sister planned it."

Sean felt a surge of awareness. Steve was so right. This game was just about as sensible as if somebody like Cheryl Suzanne, who didn't know a thing about sports, was calling the plays. "She doesn't even know about conversions or field goals," he said aloud.

"Who doesn't?" Somehow, Cheryl was on the bench

beside him once again. "Want a lick?" She offered him a taste of her everlasting ice-cream bar. Of course, she was buying another one each time she finished one. Wasn't she?

"Make tracks," he said. "This game is for men. The team will throw you out."

"Huh, nobody's noticed me," said Cheryl. She was right. All eyes were watching the fifth-grade girl cheerleaders self-consciously take the field in their deep-cut leotards and leg warmers to do aerobic drills between halves. They looked cold all over except for their knees.

Margie was there, of course, talking as usual through her gum to her best friends, Gayle and Rhonda. They all ducked up and down and waved their pom-poms. Sean wondered if she'd had any takers yesterday afternoon for her X-rated TV session.

He decided to ignore Cheryl. If he moved down the bench, it would show her that she was getting to him. She'd probably follow and stir up a fuss.

She licked away. "What are conversions and field goals?"

Even a Martian must know more than this girl! Why, Kelly had taught him football plays when he was only four years old! But this was sports talk, at least. It wasn't so bad talking to Cheryl if he explained something important.

Still, Sean tried not to look at her as he talked. "And a field goal means three points. Touchdowns are worth more, but sometimes one little field goal breaks a big tie. A conversion is a point after touchdown. You have to

30

kick it over the bar between the goalposts. You can run the ball over, like I did for two points, if you're extra lucky."

"Oh," said Cheryl Suzanne. "I guessed right."

Like a bolt of lightning, a suspicion zipped through Sean's mind. Dumb as Cheryl was about football, every time he had explained a play to her, the game that followed seemed to favor his team and especially himself.

The cheerleaders danced through another number. Black-haired Rhonda got out of step when the phonograph jiggled over the loudspeaker, but Margie nudged her back to the beat. Then they led the parents and lower graders in a cheer for the Blues.

From the corner of his eyes, Sean saw the expression on Cheryl's face. She wore a look of envy as she watched the girls. Did she really want to be like them? Well, what was keeping her?

When the cheerleaders finished, Margie took the long way back to the stands, posing prettily in her leotards and gooseflesh. Sean noticed a small, white rectangle in the middle of her back. At the same time, he caught a knowing smile on Cheryl's face.

Now it was time for the second half. Cheryl left the bench without a word. Sean forgot all about her. His mind was completely locked on the game.

The teams gathered at the middle of the field again. The Blues were receiving this time. Mike caught the ball and raced forward until it seemed he must surely be tackled. Then he lateraled the ball to Sean. It was neatly

31

delivered, and Sean ran it himself. The Greens were more alert, but Sean zigged past the last man and skidded into the end zone.

The Blues made the conversion. Sean held his breath as Mike's kick wobbled in the air currents, as direction-less as a balloon, until it finally soared just over the goalposts. The score was now fifteen to ten.

The Greens didn't look so big and tough anymore. They looked like tired and disappointed fifth graders, struggling to keep their feelings under control.

The Blues, on the other hand, just couldn't do any-thing wrong—except Mike. He fumbled twice more, but each time Sean was in the right spot to recover.

On one fourth down, Sean found himself surrounded by Green players. They were reaching too close for the punt that would have the ball deep in his own territory. He held the ball low, one hand forward, one behind, and looked for an opening. Just a little daylight showed at the knee level of two blocking linemen. Sean dropped the ball, and as it touched the grass, his toe lifted it between the players. It rose fast and high, past all the outstretched hands, on and on.

"Field goal!" shouted Coach Donlou, jumping up and down.

The final score was twenty-eight to ten. Sean's team-mates pounded his back. Never in all his dreams had he played so well.

Margie ran up in all her gooseflesh, posing and pout-ing to get Sean's attention. "You missed a good movie yesterday," she said, rolling her eyes. "It was really *a-a-a-a-dult*!"

Sean was saved from making a reply when the team teased *Margie* instead of him. The white rectangle sticking to her back was one of the stickers his mother had printed for him. Had it dropped out of his desk yesterday?

**I LOOK LIKE THIS BECAUSE
I AM A HELPLESS, NEGLECTED CHILD
WHOSE MOTHER WORKS.**

The congratulations of his teammates made Sean feel wonderful. "Wow, what speed!" crowed Dino, nearly choking Sean with his long arms in a whooping hug. "Man, you got style!"

Speed and style. "She said I could do it," thought Sean. How did she know? And why did he feel a little guilty about all this praise?

Across the field, Cheryl Suzanne was just a skinny fifth grader, a bit lost and apart from the happy groups of families and friends. Her ice-cream bar was gone. As Sean watched, she tossed the stick into the bin. She turned homeward.

Suddenly, Sean didn't want to stick around either. Swinging his blue helmet by the strap, he walked off the field.

A little kid at the curb looked up at him and said, "Hi, Sean," with worship in his voice.

"Hi." Sean walked faster. He caught sight of a lone figure walking ahead. Where does she live? he wondered. Without thinking, he followed.

V

The Growing Suspicion

Sean had been up and down these streets often before. He liked the half-grown palm trees, two on the parkway between every driveway. He liked the houses, all nearly new, pleasant, two-story homes that had been built about the time Sean entered kindergarten. Only one house in the entire neighborhood had been there before the tract builders came. People still said it was a pity that such an old eyesore should be allowed to remain in an up-to-date neighborhood. Instead of palms, it had twisted junipers and a shaggy sycamore tree.

As Cheryl Suzanne walked past the first block of newer houses, Sean had a dawning suspicion. He stopped as she turned the next corner, waiting to let her get on ahead. Then, peering around the corner hedge, he saw her, nearly a city block away, warily ducking from the view of the windows as she slipped along the side wall of the old, three-story house with dormer windows and shutters.

It was Miss Windemere's house!

Miss Windemere was the familiar-looking, gray-haired woman who had enrolled Cheryl yesterday.

What was it the kids said about Miss Windemere? Sean had sung it himself when he was a little kid, but not anymore, now that he was nearing eleven.

> Old lady witch
> Fell in a ditch,
> Picked up a penny
> And thought she was rich.

Nowadays, nobody believed in witches. Not anybody. But, if you *could* believe in witches, Miss Windemere would be a good example for a start.

So Cheryl Suzanne Endor lived with Miss Windemere! She lived in a gray, old house with a gray, old lady. A *weird* old lady.

A shiver ran through him. No wonder she was so strange—living with a witch's family!

"Speed and style," she had said. "Is that all it takes? You're as good as Mike."

And he *had* been as good as Mike. Even better.

But not without help.

Not without a spell cast by a— Was Cheryl Suzanne Endor a witch?

Oh, no. Of course not.

Now the day turned even more chill. A gust of wind bent the palm trees and blew the first dry leaf from Miss Windemere's tall sycamore along the sidewalk almost to Sean's feet.

Was she a witch?

VI

The Fabulous Field Trip

By Monday morning, Sean convinced himself that Saturday's game had been just plain luck. Still, he woke with a feeling of doom. The birdsong outside and the soft rays of sunlight inside told him that it was a lovely October day. So why did he feel so bad?

He turned over in bed. Then it struck him. The field trip! The awful, all-day field trip, trapped next to a girl— to Cheryl Suzanne. He wasn't ready for a girlfriend. He didn't want any more teasing.

He was sick.

That was it, he was sick. He lay still as a statue and investigated himself. Wasn't his head a bit achy? His tooth, maybe? His ear? What about his throat? Didn't it feel raspy? Try as he would, he couldn't feel any pain. His stomach, then? Wasn't it a little fluttery? Wouldn't Mom want to keep him home because of a food upset?

Finding no strange sensations, although he concentrated hard to cause some, Sean checked his fingers and toes. No sprains, no cramps. He felt miserably well and

36

just a bit relieved. To keep Mom home from her shop just because he imagined he felt icky really wasn't fair. Of course, he might grow suddenly woozy at bell time. Then he could snooze in the nurse's office all morning.

He grumbled to himself as he dressed. It would be different if they were going anyplace but to County Museum. County Museum had been interesting—once. Even twice. But every year—five times since he had been in kindergarten—Sean's teachers had set up a field trip to County Museum. They always got carried away with how terrific it was, but enough was enough. When you had seen the hall of mammals twice, the dinosaurs three times, the Indians, and even the mummy four times over, you got fed up.

Then there was Miss Jellenich's babyish setup. She had to call the groups by special names. Because they were studying American history and geography, she thought it clever to call Mike's group the Stagecoachers and Sean's group the Conestogans. Some fun. With her little-kid name tags, she must have expected her husky fifth graders to get lost like kindergartners. Fifth graders only got lost on purpose.

But Miss Jellenich had had them trace silhouettes of covered wagons or stagecoaches on brown paper during art time. Much as Sean liked art, he didn't think that printing his name with marking pen on a cutout badge produced a blue-ribbon masterpiece.

Mom looked in on her way to work. "I left your bran on the table. Hurry up, favorite son."

Then the house was silent. Sean peeled off his pajamas and pulled on his clothes.

He hoped the cafeteria box lunches held something good this time. Some kids got to hang around the museum lunch stands and souvenir counters, but not those from Room 6. Miss Jellenich didn't believe in bringing extra money for treats and stuff. She called field trips "study trips." "This is *not* Disneyland," she admonished. "Your parents will be disappointed if we are not learning something required for fifth grade." Huh! He bet she hadn't consulted *any* parents about how they felt.

Sean ate his cereal gloomily, set his dish and spoon in the dishwasher, and locked the front door carefully as he left.

He walked the long way past the park to avoid meeting Cheryl Suzanne. At least he wouldn't have to put up with her company longer than necessary. Maybe Cheryl Suzanne would be absent today herself. But no such luck. On field trip days, nobody was ever absent or late. Even a dull, old museum trip beat an ordinary day in class.

Usually only one or two children were gathered near the classroom door when the bell rang. Today they formed their two rows, boys and girls, seconds after the buzzer sounded. Miss Jellenich called them "inside row" and "outside row" instead of boys' line and girls' line, because that was sexist. But anybody standing in the wrong place was hooted and teased all day.

The chattering stopped as Miss Jellenich came around the corner. She had Mike's mother with her and was talking in that special, stagey voice she reserved for visitors and parents.

"Yes, the children will be ready to leave right after the flag salute and roll call. Mike is well organized. His group—both groups—know exactly how to behave. They regard their study trip as serious business, not just another holiday." Miss Jellenich was a bit of a dreamer.

It started at flag salute. Exactly on "One nation, under God, indivisible," three electronic watches went off together. Steve, Dino, and Margie looked very innocent. Miss Jellenich, already chalk-dusty, turned red.

Roll call was quick. It was easy to see nobody was missing.

Cheryl Suzanne, wearing a gray—no, a red, white, and blue dress, looked healthy and cheerful. As Sean passed out his Conestoga tags, including a straight pin for each, he started to smile at her. Then he remembered that she was the reason today was going to be so rotten. "Thank you," said Cheryl Suzanne. He hoped the pin stuck her.

She didn't seem to notice that he wasn't speaking. "Aren't field trips fun!"

Patiently, he shut her up. "Not another old trip to the old museum," he said, and then muttered under his breath, "with an old girl to sit by."

Cheryl pressed her lips together thoughtfully. "Do you suppose today might be a little *different*?"

"Leaders!" called Miss Jellenich. "Line your teams by partners. Check off everyone. We will have another checkpoint when you leave the bus, and again when we eat lunch and when we get back on to go home." Sean knew the story about the child who had hidden in the rest room at the zoo. Miss Jellenich's bus had had to turn around and go back to find her.

Sean dutifully counted the Conestogans and drew a little check mark after each name. Simple as sardines! But when Mike counted *his* group, Mike's mother seemed to be beside herself with pride that her boy could do such a difficult thing with only a little help. She looked the Stagecoachers over approvingly as each answered, "Here."

Mrs. Donlou had long, curved, red fingernails and blue eyelids, and she wore clothes a lot like Sean's own mother's, only tighter.

As Joe answered to his name, Mrs. Donlou looked him over. Joe was wearing a bright, new T-shirt that showed his clean elbows and his smudgy, penciled hands. Mrs. Donlou tapped Mike lightly and leaned across to whisper to Miss Jellenich.

"Sean," said Miss Jellenich quietly, "Joe will go with the Conestogans today. Just add his name to your list." Joe, unperturbed, obediently moved over. Mrs. Donlou took out a little comb and fussed with Mike's hair while he finished calling the names.

Getting lined up was slow because some of the children decided to leave their jackets after Miss Jellenich declared that she would not be a clothes rack whenever they felt too warm. The two files of children, ready at last, chattered happily, peering into each open classroom doorway at the poor stay-at-homes while marching past to the waiting yellow bus.

Oh-oh. Sean might have known. Number 17. The bus driver was Mrs. Grimp again. Mrs. Grimp was shaped like a large sack of cement. Mrs. Grimp did not like children. Sean often thought that if a child sneezed on her bus, Mrs. Grimp would give the whole class a bad mark for the trip.

The children sensed that Mrs. Grimp, never especially cheerful, was in one of her bad moods. Sean was glad that every child, even Margie, was silent. Mike's mother, however, chattered away to Mike and Miss Jellenich, who looked a little strained as she kept glancing at Mrs. Grimp.

Mike's group got on first, so Mike chose the right side of the bus. The Stagecoachers filled the seats in twos. Mike got to sit by his mother. Then Sean led the Conestogans onto the bus. It was humiliating enough to sit across the aisle from the Donlous. But it was real torture to share a seat with Cheryl Suzanne.

As every teacher had done since kindergarten, Miss Jellenich stood a moment at the front of the bus before she found a seat near the middle. She reminded the children that they were ladies and gentlemen. She told them that all the children in the school, and in the entire county, were being measured by how they behaved today. She hoped that they would be orderly and quiet, would hold any conversation to a whisper, would not turn around to talk to anyone behind them, and positively would not chew gum or sunflower seeds.

It was quiet except for the rustle of sunflower seed packets in several pockets. Sean noticed that Margie's jaws stopped moving up and down for a whole minute.

As soon as Miss Jellenich was seated, the bus pulled ahead. Sean knew the route very well. Go up Hawthorne

41

Boulevard to the San Diego Freeway, then go east to join Harbor Freeway and north to County Museum. Mrs. Grimp always went that way.

But today, soon after she took the San Diego on ramp, Mrs. Grimp got boxed into an inner lane by a cluster of cars. So Sean was not surprised when Mrs. Grimp drove right past the Harbor Freeway exit.

Because Sean wasn't allowed to talk (and who'd want to talk to Cheryl Suzanne, anyway?), he tried to outguess Mrs. Grimp. Where would she turn off to get back to the Harbor Freeway?

It was hard to guess. Mrs. Grimp prepared to move the bus to the off-ramp lane time after time. Just when it seemed she was ready to edge right, a cluster of on-coming cars blocked her way and forced her to the left once more.

Others were noticing, too, but it seemed no one wanted to ask questions. The big mirror above Mrs. Grimp's head reflected her damp, perplexed face.

The stream of cars beside them, as close together as beads on a necklace, finally opened to let the bus move over. To Sean's relief, Mrs. Grimp drove smoothly in the outer lane until she poured out with the cars onto *Garden Grove Freeway*! Was Mrs. Grimp taking them to the museum by way of New York?

All the children were watching now. So were Mrs. Donlou and Miss Jellenich. The bus driver clutched the steering wheel as if trying to prevent it from doing its own thing. But, of course, that was silly. Or had the power steering gone off?

Mrs. Grimp's reflected face got redder and redder. Finally, she seemed to relax her grip a little and let the bus steer itself. Now the bus purred along faster than ever.

Not a sound, not even a whisper from Margie, cut the stillness. Except for the purring motor, the bus was silent. All the children and the three grown-ups seemed to be waiting—just waiting to find out where they were going.

The bus moved back again to the outside lane and swung itself onto—not Harbor *Freeway,* but *Harbor Boulevard!*

Then the landscape began to look familiar to Sean. Above the shops and houses rose a high, white triangle, too odd-shaped to be anything but itself. "The Matterhorn!" he said to himself, but not a sound escaped his lips. "We're on our way to Disneyland!"

For the first time since he got on the bus, Sean turned to look at Cheryl Suzanne. She was wearing a soft little smile.

Sean looked back at the driver as the bus turned into a very familiar, mile-wide parking lot. Mrs. Grimp's face was now purple. Smiling attendants waved the bus onward until it drew up right at the entrance. There the motor stopped.

Mrs. Grimp turned the key and pushed buttons, but nothing would start up. Finally, she just pushed the lever to open the door and then slumped in frustration over the wheel.

As they poured out of the bus, the children suddenly

found their voices. They gazed upward. All across the entrance gate was a broad streamer reading:

FIFTH-GRADE DAY   FREE ADMISSION

Looking strained and anxious, Miss Jellenich tried to calm the children, but it was a hopeless task. "Well," she seemed to be mumbling to herself, "I can call it a lesson about America's frontier. It's time for me to sign up for a sabbatical." To the children she said over and over, "One o'clock. Be back at the bus at one o'clock!"

Disneyland had never been more fun. The lines were shorter and the rides longer than Sean had ever seen. Tom Sawyer's island was larger and more overgrown and primitive. The cave was deeper and spookier. Cheryl Suzanne followed him just like Becky Thatcher.

They climbed to the top of the Swiss Family Robinson tree house, and Cheryl made friends with a real monkey who raced to her from the highest limb.

"He doesn't usually live here," she said. "He's on leave from the Los Angeles Zoo."

No matter where Sean chose to go, Cheryl Suzanne was everywhere he turned. But he didn't mind. She rode the monorail in the same car. Didn't it run higher and farther than ever before? They could see for miles and miles.

She was right behind him on the Caribbean boat ride when one of the pirates handed them a rum bottle filled with cola and a necklace of raspberry-flavored "rubies."

44

She sat beside him down Space Mountain. They tunneled through whirling galaxies for light-years of time.

When they jumped out again, Sean remembered he was a leader and looked around for the rest of the Conestogans. They and the Stagecoachers were everywhere, having fun, too. Even Miss Jellenich was having a marvelous time making notes about the Lincoln robot. Mrs. Grimp was deep in conversation with Goofy. Joe was on the Jungleland ride, getting sprayed with water from the waterfall and laughing, as if for the first time in his life he really liked getting clean.

Margie spent most of her time in the telephone exhibit, dialing numbers all over the United States. Dino and George and Steve swooped down the Matterhorn seventeen times.

Sean wondered why he hadn't seen Mike and his mother all morning. He finally saw them at twelve twenty. They were stuck halfway across Tomorrowland in a Skyride gondola. As Sean stood there wondering what to do, a buzzer sounded all over the park. "Free lunch!" a loudspeaker announced.

The children raced to the food machines and the lunch stands to get sandwiches and tacos and ice cream and candy and sodas. Sean looked at Cheryl, who was still tagging along. "We can't eat until we get Mike and his mother down."

"Why not?" asked Cheryl, studying the buttons on a sandwich machine.

Didn't she *know*? Teasing them was one thing, but

45

you just don't *hurt* your enemies for pleasure. Sean waited, wondering how to explain.

"You're right, I guess." Cheryl snapped her fingers. "Anyway, aren't those sky cars moving now?"

Sure enough, all the empty sky cars glided past the platform until finally the Donlous' gondola stopped and let Mike and his mother out. Mike raced down the ramp to the nearest food machine. His mother joined him. For some reason, the tastiest items wouldn't come out for them. They finally had to settle for peanut butter on brown bread and plain buttermilk.

Over their own roast turkey sandwiches and frozen chocolate-covered bananas, Cheryl looked defiantly at Sean. "Well, they *did* get down in time to eat, didn't they?" she asked.

Sean didn't answer. He was trying not to think too much.

Then everyone lined the street to watch the parade. It was great fun being in the front row and able to see every noisy float.

"Bus time!" blared the loudspeaker.

All the children reluctantly found their leaders. Mike and his mother were very short-tempered with the Stage-coachers, who had all had a much better time than their captain. Sean felt smug and happy as the Conestogans lined up obediently, chattering about the exciting morning.

Both groups marched crisply behind stern-faced Mrs. Grimp to the bus. Miss Jellenich, bringing up the rear, wore a faint frown in spite of the smile that kept tugging at her mouth. Looking back, Sean could see that she was worrying. What would Mr. Drake say when Mike's mother came in to tell him what had happened?

Now all the children seemed to have that same thought. They were silent as they filed back on the bus. Mike went in with his group, followed by Sean and the Conestogans, but Mrs. Donlou stayed outside the door and scolded Miss Jellenich.

The children could hear every word. "Miss Jellenich, I am certainly going to tell the principal how you deceived us. You said you were taking the children on an educational trip to the County Museum, but all the time you had arranged to take them to—"

Everyone waited, but the word wouldn't come out. Mrs. Donlou couldn't say *Disneyland*!

"Mr. Drake will be very unhappy about the way you have wasted the taxpayers' money. The taxpayers expected you to go to the museum. But, instead, you went to the—the museum?" Mrs. Donlou looked very surprised at her own words.

Sean had an urge to say *Disneyland*, too. "I sure had a good time," he began, "at—*the museum*!" The other children heard him and tried to say it themselves.

"I simply love to ride the monorail at *the museum*!" they squealed. "The submarine was sure exciting at *the museum*!" They rocked with laughter. "The museum Trip to the Atom! The museum Frontierland!" No one seemed able to say the true destination of their trip.

Sean found himself watching Mrs. Grimp in her mirror. The expression on the driver's face had been solemn and embarrassed while Mrs. Donlou talked with Miss Jellenich. As Mrs. Donlou got more and more mixed up, Mrs. Grimp's expression grew more and more pleasant.

"Come in, ladies," she said, reaching for the key. The motor purred flawlessly, as if it promised to give no more trouble. "We have to hustle to get home from the museum on time."

Mrs. Donlou came in huffily and sat down by Mike. Miss Jellenich followed serenely.

The ride home was quiet with contentment. Everyone but Mike and his mother seemed drowsy and happy. The Donlous looked like two storm clouds that had no place to rain.

Sean glanced sideways at Cheryl Suzanne. Why had he ever disliked her? On some of those rides today, she had been a lot of fun. She turned now and met his eye.

"Did you like going to the same old museum on an old field trip with an *old girl*?" she asked innocently.

Sean's face broke into a grin. "It sure *was* different! How in heck did you know what would happen?"

Cheryl shrugged as if it were the most natural thing in the world to know ahead when something odd would take place, like today at Disneyland or Saturday at the football game.

But it wasn't natural. And it wasn't luck, not when Cheryl Suzanne Endor was along. Sean didn't doubt it anymore.

48

"Witch!" he whispered.

"Well, not really. Just an apprentice. I'm still under eleven." She snuggled her knees up onto the seat. "And I can't really do much without Aunty's pentagram." She patted her pocket. "I think I'll take a nap."

Apprentice witch!

VII

Halloween Hoaxing

Strangely, back at school the rest of the day, nobody talked about the unusual study trip. When Sean asked Dino, "What did you like best?" Dino looked a little forgetful and wrinkled his forehead in thought.

"I dunno. The mummy, I guess."

At football practice, Sean checked what the other kids remembered. Nobody seemed to recall a thing out of the ordinary. Even Mike had tuned out his bad day. "Field trips are dumb, and so are you."

But Sean didn't forget, not a bit. These kids *had* been to Disneyland today and ought to remember everything about it! Cheryl Suzanne had made them all forget. But not Sean!

Sean found himself pulled more and more to Cheryl. So she was an apprentice witch! Was it all right to like an apprentice witch? Most people didn't even *believe* in witches.

He sounded out his family. "Dad," Sean asked his father before dinner as they hauled the potted ivy and fern plants out into the driveway to catch the promised rain, "is it okay to believe in witches?"

"I'm not very good on witches," said Dad, hoisting the heavy ceramic pot. "I'm better on birds and bees."

"We had *that* talk last month," Sean reminded him. "Let's stick to witches. Do you believe in them?"

"Evil eye? Stuff like that? No, I don't."

"Why not?"

"Fourteen units of college science, mostly. Why?"

"Nothing. Well, yes . . . there's this new girl in my room. . . ." His voice trailed off as though something held back his words.

Dad waited. Then he grinned. "A girl, is it? In that case, I believe in witches. And in birds and bees. Let a woman come into your life and she'll bewitch you. You're sunk, kid. Fourteen units of college science won't help a bit. Try garlic."

"That's for werewolves. Well, thanks anyway."

Inside, Sean found his mother on the stepladder hanging the freshly washed curtains. "Don't tell the neighbors you caught me being domestic," she said, "or I'll lose my NOW membership."

"Mom, what do you think about witches?"

"I admire them a lot. Not much for style, and most of them need nose jobs, but they're movers and shakers. Why?"

"Do you think witches can really change things? Cast spells? Stuff like that?"

His mother climbed down the ladder and gave him a hug. "I'm not much for horoscopes. I like to think *every-*

body changes things—a little or a lot. Everybody. Not just witches. Even *you*. Now that you wash behind your ears faithfully, you're positively enchanting."

"Awwwww," said Sean modestly, "I bet you say that to all your handsome sons. Anyway, would *you* be a friend to a witch who casts spells?"

"Does she need a friend?"

"Oh, yes."

"I make it a rule," said Mrs. Wilkerson, folding the ladder, "never to give advice to people who already know the answers. I'd say she's a very lucky witch." The microwave oven dinged. "Call Dad for dinner."

They ate. Then Sean helped Kelly clean up. Kelly's questions were more direct, but, after Sean's first careful words, his tongue didn't hold back his answers. "Can you tell me why she casts her spells?" Kelly asked. "Is it to make people happy?"

"Not always," Sean said reluctantly, remembering the Donlous in the sky car.

"Is it to be mean?"

"Uhhh—mostly to set people straight."

"Does it work?"

"Not so far. But it's kinda fun to watch them squirm."

Kelly's mouth twitched. "Bring Cheryl Suzanne to see me sometime. Promise?"

"I promise," said Sean.

It rained all Monday night. The TV announcers made a big thing of the weather and showed satellite cloud pictures and wet pedestrians. On Tuesday morning, all the children in Room 6 came to school bundled in new padded jackets or parkas. They hung their wraps inside the portable closet along the side wall. By recess time, the clouds were gone and everyone went outside in shirt sleeves.

Miss Jellenich was excited now about the Oregon Trail, but all that the kids talked about was Halloween.

Deciding what to be on Halloween was half the fun. The little kids all wore costumes from the drugstore, but fifth graders took pride in being original.

At odd moments, Sean found himself wondering whether to be a prospector with Gramps' old boots and a frying pan or a ghost in a white sheet if he could find one, or a hobo, or a corrugated cardboard computer.

Mike Donlou, naturally, had a brand-new robot suit. "It cost forty-five dollars," Mike told everybody. "It isn't cheap and homemade."

This year, Steve planned to be a break dancer in tank top and cutoffs, and three of the Room 6 girls were dressing like their favorite video stars. Dino had a gorilla suit.

"I know what Joe can be," teased Margie. "He can wash his face and comb his hair and be a complete stranger!"

"And you can keep quiet for once and be a broken TV set," said Joe.

"Children," chided Miss Jellenich. "This is math and not recess. If we work hard every day this week, I won't need to give homework on Halloween night."

The class cheered. Margie said, "Just for that, Miss

Jellenich, I'll bring you some of my candy the day after Halloween."

"If I get any licorice," said George, "you can have it all."

"Sweets for the sweet!" caroled Mike, making Miss Jellenich flinch.

They settled down to work. When the bell sounded, Cheryl Suzanne followed Sean out to recess. She called him as he reached the brick handball backboard. He stopped in its shadow to talk.

"Sean, what is 'trick and treat'?"

"Trick *or* treat," Sean corrected. "Where've you been since you were born? That's when you knock on people's doors on Halloween night and they divvy up candy or plastic junk to keep you from playing a trick."

"Do you have to knock every time you play a trick? What kind of trick?"

"I don't know," said Sean honestly. "I never had to play one. I always get candy."

"Why do you want candy?"

"Keech!" said Sean. For this he was missing out on handball. She might as well ask why he breathed! "Not everyone hands out candy. The corner neighbor gives dinky boxes of crayons. Some people give combs or pencils. Margie's mother gives gum." He shook his head at her ignorance. "What do *you* do on Halloween? Your homework?"

"Why not? Oh, you're joking. Well, Halloween is important to us, but my aunts don't believe in things like going out for candy."

"I understand," said Sean, nodding. "I eat up half my loot before I get home, 'cause Mom throws out the good stuff. Are your aunts hipped on nutrition, too?"

"Nutrition?"

"That's the stuff you have to eat before you earn any dessert," explained Sean. "If your family doesn't let you go out to ring doorbells, what *do* you do on Halloween?" As he waited for her reluctant answer, he had a strong surge of curiosity. Whatever Cheryl did for Halloween, it would be a night of witchcraft, for sure!

Cheryl Suzanne looked about nervously. The handball game had the attention of everyone nearby. "*I* don't do much of anything," she finally admitted.

Sean waited.

"But *they* meet in a coven."

"*They?*"

"My aunts and their friends."

"What's a coven?"

"Thirteen witches and wizards. There must be exactly thirteen for esbaths—that's a kind of business meeting whenever there's something to decide—and for regular celebrations, too. There's a Candlemas party in February, and Roodmas in May, and Lammas in August, and then All Hallows' Eve. They *have* to celebrate with parties."

"Are the parties for kids, too? Do you ask any friends?"

Cheryl looked scared. "Aunts are different from parents. Aunts think children are too childish."

"Don't they let you come in like the other guests? You're a witch, too."

"Oh, no. I told you, I'm just an apprentice. The coven

is only for grown-ups. I sometimes get to serve them tea, but mostly I just climb partway down the stairs and peek through the rails."

"Trick or treat is more fun," Sean declared. "I like going house to house."

"I s'pose," said Cheryl, looking bleak. "But *I* never visit in other people's houses. My aunts—well, we just don't. Besides," she added haughtily, "who needs candy? All you have to do is *think* candy and even a dill pickle will taste like divinity fudge."

"I'm not that good a thinker."

"Well, I *do* have to work a teeny spell."

"*I*," said Sean, with wry truthfulness, "am a very poor speller." When Cheryl had no answer, he went on. "Besides, it's fun for people you know to guess who's behind the mask."

"But then you have to wear a costume." Cheryl looked wistful. "Aunt Laura says it's always wise to dress in-con-spic-u-ous-ly."

"If she doesn't want you to be noticed, why do you change your gray dresses to colored ones at recess every day?"

"Joe asked me that, too," said Cheryl. "He likes the gray ones." Her voice dropped to a whisper. "Aunt Laura doesn't know. I change without permission. I just think pink with my help-spell. Or red, white, and blue." A shadow of worry crossed her face.

"I won't tell your aunt," Sean reassured her. "I won't tell anyone you don't want to know."

Cheryl's frown vanished. "It's all right that *you* know

56

I can do things like that. But witches have sometimes been treated badly just for being witches. Aunt Laura just said to be sure that none of my girl friends ever learns about me. As if any of the girls ever wanted to know. . . . Anyway, Aunty didn't say a word about not telling a boy."

Sean felt that there was something faulty in Cheryl's reasoning, but he didn't tell her so. "Let's get a drink."

Cheryl followed. "I do wish I had some girl friends. But you're the only friend I've made since I came here for fifth grade."

As if to prove her point, Cheryl indicated Margie and Gayle and Rhonda walking toward them. Dark-haired Rhonda saw them and seemed about to speak, but Sean saw Margie's elbow nudge her to be silent.

Sean wasn't sure who stuck her nose in the air last, Cheryl or Rhonda, but all four girls seemed to be looking for airplanes until the three walked on past.

Sean felt bad. Cheryl didn't know how to get along with girls at all. Should he ask her to come with him and Dino and Steve on Halloween night? What would the boys do? More teasing for sure. And it might embarrass her.

He wondered what Kelly would suggest. That was it!

"You ought to meet my sister, Kelly," Sean declared. "She wants to meet you. And you don't have to go to my house. We can stop by The Slinkery during her shift. She may even find something with calories in it for us to munch."

Cheryl considered his suggestion. "I don't know what

Aunt Laura would say about a restaurant. That's not exactly like a house. Anyway," Cheryl said firmly, "Kelly won't like me."

"Don't flinch before you're hit." Sean was a little irritated at Cheryl himself.

"Well, Margie and most of the girls always gush over fads or fashions or boys. They say what clothes to wear and what people to like. I'm not like them."

"Neither is Kelly. Look. I don't have practice tonight. We can jog to The Slinkery after school in ten minutes." He waited.

Cheryl gulped and nodded.

Kelly would see ways to smooth things for Cheryl. And if Cheryl didn't listen, why should Sean worry about her? He'd go out treating with the boys and forget about her. Feeling concern for Cheryl Suzanne might mess up a good time.

"If I see your sister, will you do me a favor?"

Hummph, thought Sean. Seeing Kelly would be fun, not a chore. "What?" he asked cagily.

"I can't visit people's houses," said Cheryl. "But I might be allowed to go outdoors on Halloween. Why not come *tricking* with me?"

"Tricking? Cheryl, my mom and dad will hit the moon if I play any tricks on the neighbors."

"How about on someone you don't know?"

"Aw, come off it, Cheryl. You don't know how to get along at all."

Cheryl turned huffy. "I was just asking you to share some fun." The wicked gleam that flared in her eye slowly turned to acceptance. "Oh, all right. What if we play just *good* tricks? Good, kind tricks. Will you come?"

"No," said Sean, nodding. He kept nodding until he realized he had actually said yes. Then he began to shake his head in disbelief. He gave in. "Don't get any idea I'm giving up all my Halloween candy because you made me say yes. I'm just going with you to please Dr. Crowley, my dentist."

The bell ended recess and they lined up. Nobody wanted to stand by Joe, who had spent recess in a mud puddle. They went in to reading class.

After school, the weather was so sunny that nearly every jacket and parka stayed behind in the portable closet when the dismissal bell rang. Sean and Cheryl jogged to The Slinkery in seven minutes and three seconds, according to Sean's digital watch.

The Slinkery had a bright service counter like other fast-food restaurants, but the resemblance ended there. Little cloth-covered tea tables and dainty chairs replaced the comfortable plastic booths Sean liked. And Kelly wore a shower-cappish bonnet and a ruffled blouse cut low enough to suit even Margie.

"Hi!" said Kelly. "You're Cheryl Suzanne. The ice cream is good today. It has fake cream and fake sugar and fake vanilla, but the ice is for real."

"I'll take steak," said Sean.

"You'll take what you get. This is *my* treat." Kelly dismissed Sean with a look and turned back to Cheryl. "I'll slather on real chocolate sauce and toss in sliced almonds for token nutrition." She chatted along as she scooped mounds of ice cream into two oval bowls and dolloped on extra toppings. "Sit there by the window."

Sean carried their tray to the window table while Cheryl stared back at Kelly and then every which way. She checked the walls and ceiling and other tables and people. "You'd think she was a tourist in a foreign country," Sean thought.

They sat and gobbled their dessert just as if it were genuine. Kelly took her break and sat, too.

"I'm really glad to meet you at last, Cheryl! You aren't quite like our ordinary customer, but you'll do fine."

" 'Ordinary'?"

"Average. In our case, overweight. But you are certainly not ordinary. And you're surely not overweight! How lucky can you get?"

"It would be nice to be ordinary—average." Cheryl spooned her last bit of ice cream in a swirl.

"Cheryl Suzanne Endor, you have to learn to be proud of being different. Nothing is duller than average!"

"I don't know," argued Sean, thinking of a recent reading test. "Sometimes a C-minus looks pretty good."

Kelly scowled at him.

"Well, it beats a D."

"Sean, pretend you're not here. This is girl talk. Cheryl Suzanne, it's pretty easy to be like everybody else, a lot easier than being different. Sometimes it's okay to go along with the crowd. But most of the time it's mighty important to be different—special—exactly who you are!"

Cheryl sat silently. Kelly checked the clock and settled back. "Cheryl, maybe you haven't given yourself enough time to find real friends. You've only been here a few weeks. And you have a wonderful talent."

"But it makes me too different. I have to practice casting spells every day—my aunts make me work at them an hour each afternoon. I do the melon seeds, and soon I'll spell the squash. I pull the draperies before I start so no one can see me. Yet people can tell I'm not like them, even if they don't know why."

"Cheryl, being different isn't being wrong. You may not be making friends because you are looking in the wrong places."

"But it was nearly the same back in Massachusetts. My aunts say that I mustn't make anybody angry. It's better not to be noticed at all, at least when you *aren't* just like everybody else. Our ancestors had enemies back in Salem. People came to them for helpful spells, but turned around and blamed them for bad things like storms or sick animals or accidents. Even last summer in Massachusetts, the neighbors began to tell stories about us. Just because Aunt Margaret's nine owls slept on the TV aerials every day, they sent for the animal shelter truck to take them all away."

"How sad for her."

Cheryl looked right and left. "It turned out all right," she whispered. "They flew out here with some Canadian geese last week. They live in our sycamore now and they keep field mice out of the squash garden. But that's why Aunt Laura insisted we move out here with her. She says that people in California are accustomed to having unusual neighbors."

"I've heard that," said Kelly. She gathered the empty dishes into a neat, carry-away stack. "Cheryl, you will argue with yourself over and over, but I hope you will always be just what you are and do what you have to do." Kelly patted her hand. "Girl talk over. Come back and see me, Cheryl. You, too, Sean, when you turn that C-minus to a C-plus."

Kelly took the dishes and raced back to her counter.

By Halloween, the spirits of the children were so high that Miss Jellenich declared time-out the last school hour. "Let's tell about our costumes for tonight. Rhonda can be the chairperson." Miss Jellenich withdrew to her desk to wait out the clock.

Sean learned nothing new except that Joe was planning to ring doorbells as a coal miner and that Mike's robot costume now cost seventy dollars. He listened, half sorry yet half excited about his agreement with Cheryl Suzanne.

At home, Sean made a last-minute decision to be a robber. In black tights borrowed from Kelly and a warm, black sweatshirt of his own, he examined his reflection in the closet mirror. The tights made his knees look knobby, so he layered them with black cutoffs. Kelly lent him her second-best eyebrow pencil to draw a thin mustache. He added a domino mask to hide his eyes.

"If the cat burglar will now eat a good supper, we'll ship him out with the other bandits," said Sean's father. "Are you old enough to stick to your own neighborhood, or will I have to walk you around again this year, too?"

"Oh, Dad." It had been three years since his father had walked up and down Diablo Drive with him on Halloween. But Sean did eat a good dinner, thinking wistfully of the gang that would be gathering soon on Dino's front lawn. They would all end up with candy, while he would have—nothing.

Sean helped clear the table and went back upstairs. He didn't want any questions about this evening's plans. He passed his mother, who had arranged to be home early to be doorkeeper. She stitched away on boutique doodads alongside the large bowl overflowing with wrapped carob bars. They were as close as Sean and Kelly had let her get to bran and granola.

Now Sean looked out his upstairs bedroom window, made hazy from dampness and the reflected lights of Los Angeles. The limbs of the eastern elm stood out more sharply against them.

"Hurry up," said Cheryl Suzanne.

Sean leaped in surprise. There, high in the elm tree where none of the kids but Sean had ever been able to climb before, sat Cheryl Suzanne. She, too, was all in black, with a skirt that draped so far over the branch on which she sat that Sean knew it came to her ankles.

"How did you—? I *am* hurrying. I'll meet you downstairs in a minute." Meet her, huh! It would take an hour for her to get down out of that tree, and then he'd have to get a ladder when she gave up and cried. He ran downstairs. " 'Bye, Mom."

Cheryl Suzanne was waiting at the door.

She wore a pointed, black hat on her black hair. The

only part of her that showed in the darkness was her white, heart-shaped face. "Hurry!" she said. "We haven't much time."

The increasing fog blurred the sky like overhead curtains, but Sean felt warm and comfortable in his lightweight costume.

"It sure gets dark fast here," complained Cheryl. "When the sun goes down, it's night. I miss twilight."

"Twilight? I thought that was only a poetry word."

"Not in Massachusetts. But tonight this darkness is fine. No one will see me come back inside when I go home."

Each streetlight was globed in mist. Up and down Diablo Drive the entranceways were patches of brilliance, with glowing pumpkins or welcoming porch lights.

Cheryl paused under a neighbor's palm tree. She looked about in delighted wonder. Looming shapes that became little children dressed as ghosts and goblins skipped and chattered along the dark sidewalk and up the paths to ring the doorbells.

Overhead, the palm fronds had made a hotel for visiting birds, still chirping as they settled for the night. "In Massachusetts, we don't hear many birds after the middle of October. They all go south," whispered Cheryl, sounding a bit homesick.

"We *are* south," said Sean.

Cheryl cocked her head and seemed to be listening. "But *these* birds are from Montana."

Sean had no answer. He changed the subject. "It's Halloween. Show me your tricks."

64

Sean didn't really want to play tricks. And he didn't completely trust Cheryl Suzanne.

"Hey!" he said, noticing a problem as they walked along the dark street. "Mrs. White left her hose out. Somebody might turn it on and leave it running or even aim it in her mail drop."

"Somebody sure might," said Cheryl cheerfully. "Wouldn't Aunt Laura have a tizzy if she guessed where I am and what I'm doing?"

Sean was instantly sorry he'd mentioned the hose. He could see the mischievous gleam lighting Cheryl's face.

"I know a good trick." Cheryl clapped her hands and raced over to the hose. In her dark costume, she was probably invisible to the masked children knocking at nearby houses. She released the hose from the faucet and held the end so that it seemed to follow her like a great snake. "Help me throw it."

Sean watched, confused. It really didn't look like she was making trouble. He picked up the second end at Cheryl's bidding.

At the same time, they threw the ends up over the limb of an elm tree, just above their reach. The hose slithered up and over, and the two ends became inter-tangled. Sean rubbed his eyes. There, above their heads where only a grown-up could get it down, the hose was tied in a beautiful bowknot, like a ribbon decorating a tree.

"That *is* a good trick!" he whispered in awe.

"Isn't a trick more fun when you can be sort of wicked, too?" crowed Cheryl.

They checked either side of the street, looking for other pleasant mischief. Sean heard an animal whimper. "Oh, it's a sweet little puppy!" exclaimed Cheryl, bending over a small, fluffy dog. "And it's lost." She picked it up and held it to her ear. "It lives down the street at the corner. Let's leave it off when we get there."

They passed Sean's gang, but no one seemed to notice them. The gorilla suit must have been hot, because Dino had his arms hanging out, so that he looked like half an octopus. Mike was not with them. He had evidently decided to get more loot by working alone.

Mr. Johnson's lawn, as usual, was high with uncut grass. His mower was beside the house, where he had left it two weeks ago to be ready when he got around to mowing. "Shall we?" asked Cheryl Suzanne. The streetlight glinted in her eyes.

Sean had started power mowers before, but he was nowhere nearly as fast as Cheryl Suzanne. She handed him the puppy, then only touched the mower, and it quietly purred. She gave it a shove onto the lawn and then leaned lazily against the house, watching the mower spin and purr and turn around.

It was the craziest kind of dance. Then the mower swooped back to them, leaned itself against the house next to Cheryl, and turned itself off.

Sean just shook his head. He handed the puppy back to Cheryl and walked beside her to the sidewalk, where they turned to admire the work. The mower had done a rather poor job of mowing, but it could spell perfectly.

66

Across the lawn like a misty streamer, the cut grass read:

"Now he'll have to mow tomorrow, and the neighbors will be pleased." Cheryl skipped a little. "Oh, what is Mike up to?"

Ahead of them, along the sidewalk where Mr. Burgess had just put in a high pine fence, stood a robot. The robot was dipping a brush into a can of white paint. As they watched, squinting, an X-rated word appeared along the length of the fence. Mr. Burgess had planned to paint on Saturday, Sean knew. The supplies were next to the barrel Mr. Burgess used to collect lawn trimmings. You could tell the barrel belonged to him because it had his house number—*1300*—neatly printed on the side.

But the fence could not wait for Saturday, not with its new decoration. Cheryl shifted the puppy and snapped her fingers.

The brush slipped from the robot's fingers. As he

reached, it flipped against him. The whole front of his robot head was streaked with white paint.

Quickly grabbing his chockful bag of treats, Mike raced for the corner. The bag tore as he dragged it, strewing candy bars and candy kisses all along the walk.

"Too bad." Cheryl didn't sound the least sorry. "Hurry," she urged Sean. "We must fix the fence." He held the open can of paint while Cheryl held the brush and the puppy. The brush fairly flew. Sean couldn't believe how fast it swooped the paint from top panel to bottom, leaving a smooth coat of white as neat as any expert could do. In five minutes, the whole fence was covered completely.

"Now we must sign our work," said Cheryl.

Sean felt a trace of guilt, but he chuckled inside. The house number on the barrel read:

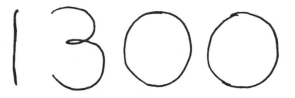

Cheryl held the brush gently and filled in three strokes. Now the house number was gone. The barrel had a new message:

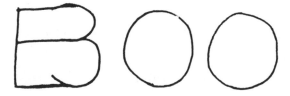

In a jiffy, the lid was back on the paint can, and the can and brush were back in place beside the barrel.

At the corner house, Cheryl Suzanne put the puppy on the porch. She didn't even touch the doorbell, but it chimed. A red-eyed woman came to the door. She didn't see Cheryl at all, just the puppy.

"Arf or arf!" said the puppy distinctly. Or was it "Trick or treat!"?

"Friday!" gasped the woman. "You're back!" she swooped the dog into her arms, cooing and crying at once. "How did you ring the bell? Did you ask for a treat? Where did you get this paint on your tail?" The door closed. Sean and Cheryl exchanged wide grins.

"It's nearly nine o'clock," said Sean as they completed the last of seventeen more good-bad tricks. "Time to get home." It had been the finest Halloween of his life. "I'll walk your way so you get home all right."

"Oh, don't bother over me. I'll just slip in without bothering my aunts. They're getting ready for their All Hallows' Eve party. They think I've stayed in my room all evening."

"Well, guys have to see that their girls are safe, like Kelly's friends do when she's been on a date."

"I don't think this is a date," murmured Cheryl, not denying that she was Sean's girl. "Well, don't come into my yard. I can climb the vine to the roof of the porch and get through the window into the house. If the kittens smell a stranger, they'll be noisy."

Sean stood outside the wooden picket fence, watching Cheryl's dim, black outline tiptoe down the path across

69

her front lawn toward the porch entrance. She was almost there when Sean felt something rub and then twist about his ankles. He looked down in the dimness to see three purring black kittens. With a smile, he bent to pet them.

And they began to bark!

With a white face, Cheryl looked back at him in dismay as a sudden strip of light widened at the door. Suddenly, she was outlined in a bright ray that glowed all the way across the lawn to where Sean stood. Both were trapped as if a camera had caught them at a crime.

"Cheryl Suzanne Endor!" said a deep alto voice, even angrier-sounding than Mr. Drake's when you'd been sent to the office for the fourth time. "Come in this house at once!"

Cheryl seemed to shrink into the darkness as she slid meekly past the tall, gray-haired woman who stood in the open doorway.

"And you, young man—you with the mustache! At this house, we do not have callers and we do not go calling. On your way!"

The door closed with a firm slam, erasing the ribbon of light. "Woof!" said one of the kittens as Sean turned away. What would happen to Cheryl now?

He dragged home, his high spirits vanished. "No candy?" asked his mother, looking up from trimming a fancy pillow.

"Candy is bad nutrition."

"Pity. I'll just have to throw out these unwanted, orphaned carob bars."

"Well, it's not *their* fault, poor things." Sean grabbed the whole bowl. "I'm going to bed." He kissed his mother.

"Your mustache doesn't tickle like your father's," she said.

"Good night, son," said Dad from his desk, pushing aside a price list to give Sean a hug.

Sean passed Kelly on the stairs. "Did you tear my tights?" she asked threateningly, then smiled over her shoulder to show she was only teasing. "Did you have fun?"

Sighing, Sean closed his bedroom door behind him. Even after he had unwrapped and chewed a carob bar, he couldn't fill the worried emptiness deep in his stomach.

Poor Cheryl Suzanne. What would her angry aunt do?

VIII

The Problem
With Parents

The guilty, hollow feeling returned to Sean's stomach when he looked at Cheryl the first school day after Halloween. She didn't say a word. Her eyes avoided his. He cornered her at first recess right outside Room 6.

"Cheryl, what—?"

" 'Scuse me," she said, dodging past him into the girls' rest room. He waited around outside and even asked Rhonda to go in and tell Cheryl to come out. But the bell rang before she appeared.

The next recess was the same, and at noon she went home for lunch, returning at the last bell.

Even at phys ed time, Sean couldn't get close to Cheryl to talk. Mr. Drake took all the boys to the grassy east playground to practice for the president's fitness test while Miss Jellenich tested the girls on the blacktop.

While Sean waited his turn at the pull-up bars, he kept looking over at the girls to check on Cheryl. The lumpier girls seemed to do better than the skinnier ones on the timed chair push-ups; they didn't have as far to go to touch the chair.

Sean tied with Mike on bar pull-ups, but when Mr. Drake had them pair off to count each other's timed sit-ups, Mike's count on Sean was five less than he'd earned. Sean held his temper—since this was only practice— but he'd manage to get another partner for the real thing.

The girls moved from the blacktop to the grass, with Cheryl trailing the others. She had no partner to hold her feet and count her sit-ups, but Sean saw Miss Jellenich motion to Rhonda to take over.

He finally caught up with Cheryl after school, but she looked anxious and miserable, and she headed for the front gate instead of cutting across the school yard to the side exit as usual. "Please, I can't talk. Especially not to you. I had to beg and beg to come back to school at all!" Then she ran past the school office to the sidewalk, right to an old-fashioned black sedan that waited at the curb. As she opened the passenger side, Sean got a glimpse of the driver. Under her skewered, gray hair, Miss Windemere's stern frown was even more glowering than Mrs. Grimp's. She turned slowly and looked straight at Sean. Her eyes were graveyard cold.

Each day, new things happened in fifth grade, but Sean could see that Cheryl's problem didn't change a bit. She stayed out of the way or just froze like a statue whenever Sean came near. At her desk, she kept her back turned away as if she wanted to shrink into invis-

73

ibility. Once he caught up with her at recess just to try to force her to talk and be friends again. The next day, she didn't come to school at all.

So, each afternoon, Sean watched the old-fashioned black sedan take Cheryl away. He felt helpless and unhappy.

Report cards and parent conferences were coming up. When Miss Jellenich handed out her letters to parents, Cheryl turned pale.

As Sean passed hers across, Cheryl fumbled and dropped it, then bent over, her flushed face half hidden by her long, lank hair. She recovered the paper and placed it facedown before her, huddling a bit as the rest of the class opened their daily journals to write.

Sean dated his page and scribbled: "Perennt confrennses comming. I better be good. I hope I get a good report. My reeding has improoved." He might have written a full page, because none of it was ever graded. Miss Jellenich occasionally stopped by to check the journals upside down, just to see that the children were using their journal time correctly. Sometimes she forced back a little smile when she saw what Sean had written. But teachers can't read upside down, can they?

Cheryl Suzanne distracted him from further writing by her stiff, withdrawn posture. He glanced at her journal. She had not written a word.

Poor Cheryl. All she needed to make her life any worse was to have Miss Windemere come for a conference,

Sean thought. He wondered what Miss Jellenich would have to say about a girl who had been in Room 6 over a month and hadn't made any friends.

"Any friends she dares talk to," he corrected himself.

Everybody liked the idea of having a shortened school day during conference time. But the only fifth grader who really wanted his parents to confer was Mike. "If I get a good report, I get to go to Magic Mountain," he said. He began bringing Miss Jellenich big apples each morning.

Sean studied Miss Jellenich. November was a rough month for her. Her hair seemed to spring loose and dangle, and it had a different color at the roots. She was wearing darker winter clothes now, and the yellow chalk dust seemed to leap to her elbows and back and even her pillowy front whenever she passed the board.

She kept a large chart of the conference openings on the side wall, but it seemed to be a struggle for her to get it filled. Most of the parent letters drifted back finally with a time and date checked. Miss Jellenich pressured the slowpokes.

"Steve, are you *sure* the only time your folks can come is eight o'clock Thursday evening? I thought your mother wasn't working this year."

"She wants Dad to come, too." Miss Jellenich looked crestfallen. She always *said* conferences were for both parents, but she relaxed more when only one parent signed to come.

"Your father's day off is Wednesday. Can he come then at two?"

"Naw. Dad likes to take it easy on his day off."

Miss Jellenich checked on another laggard. "Dino?"

"Mama will come anytime, anytime. Can she bring my baby brother?" Miss Jellenich nodded, delighted to fill a blank. "Mama don' speak English."

"Uh—does your father speak English?"

Dino shrugged and spread his arms. "*I* do." Sean watched Dino set up another conference as interpreter, just as he had last year. It was very convenient for Dino to edit his own report, and no teacher ever knew that Mr. Mario, who never came, was fluent in English.

Eventually, all the parent letters but Cheryl's and Margie's had safely returned. Sean was glad Miss Jellenich didn't keep bugging Cheryl, who had troubles enough. He didn't mind about Margie. When pressed, Margie said she was sure her letter had come back the second day. "I handed it to you at math time," she insisted, but she didn't exactly remember the day and hour her mother had written down. She agreed to take another copy home, then explained at length that none of the empty spaces left on Miss Jellenich's wall chart was convenient.

"We can't meet during class time," objected Miss Jellenich. "Wait a minute after school and I'll write a separate note."

"Oh, I can't wait tonight," said Margie, and at least five classmates nodded to confirm. "My folks need me home fast. That's why I ride my bike."

Sean was curious to see who would win—Margie or Miss Jellenich. Probably Margie. He had noticed that more and more of the children clustered around her at recess, and a parade of bicycles followed her right after dismissal. "Coming, Sean?" she asked as she left each day, rolling her eyes and giggling.

"I like the sports channel better," he said.

When conferences finally started, every day was like a holiday. Miss Jellenich had explained that the children were not being given a free hour—it was really home study time. Sean noticed that nobody ever showed up smarter the next day.

For two weeks, Miss Jellenich looked different. Instead of her usual low shoes and culottes and two-toned hair, she wore heels and dresses and a shiny, tight frizz. Whatever she wore underneath held her middle in a lot more than usual; she didn't bounce so much when she was partner to anybody left over in folk dancing.

Miss Jellenich acted differently, too. She grew more and more short-tempered. It started with Joe. Today she wore a white knit dress. To dictate the social studies test, she sat on the empty side of Joe's table. At noon, she had to drive home to change her clothes.

"Joe, why *do* you mark pencil lead on every surface?"

"I like the color," said Joe, reasonably.

So all of the kids except Cheryl hung around after early dismissal just to see Miss Jellenich's face when she met Joe's mother. Waiting for the first appointment of the afternoon was a tall, beautiful woman who looked like a TV star. Below the open window, Margie eavesdropped and then told all.

"You know what used to be Joe's favorite game? Mud pies!"

Dino himself shared what went on in Mrs. Mario's conference. He really liked going along. Everybody was so happy. His baby brother had a good time eating chalk; Miss Jellenich seemed pleased because Dino's mother took all the bad news so well; and Mrs. Mario was delighted that Dino was the finest boy in Room 6.

At first, Sean was a little uneasy about his own conference. His folks had already seen his C's in reading and spelling, but the social studies B and the A's in phys ed and work habits seemed to balance things out. He was kind of proud of the way his parents looked whenever they came to school. Mom wore her best blazer and skirt, and Dad trimmed his beard to its most dignified. Even if Miss Jellenich had something unpleasant to tell them at their early-morning meeting, whatever she said was pretty well forgotten by dinnertime.

Miss Jellenich was so busy with parents that she dithered and fussed the class time away. She promised less math and more art as soon as the school day lengthened. "We'll decorate the room and make presents to give during the winter holidays." Miss Jellenich was careful to allow equal time for everybody's winter celebration. "I'll order pottery clay from Mr. Drake this week." Now and then, she would glance worriedly at Cheryl, frown at Margie, and say, "I am still waiting for two conference responses."

The cafeteria switched to catered box lunches. For a few days, everybody ate them for the novelty. Sean noticed that Mike collected the tiny envelopes of salt left

78

over at his table. Later in the classroom, Mike slipped behind Rhonda, the girl with the darkest hair, and salted her scalp. She didn't even notice.

A few minutes passed. Then, acting a bit surprised at what he noticed as he passed Rhonda's chair on his way to get a drink, Mike changed his route and went to whisper quietly to Miss Jellenich.

Sean couldn't hear what Mike said, but he watched Miss Jellenich rise from correcting social studies notebooks and casually walk over to glance at Rhonda's parted hair.

After recess, the school nurse was waiting. She used little Popsicle sticks to check every head in the room. When she came to Rhonda, she looked shocked and then amused. She went out smiling. "Better safe than sorry," she said to Miss Jellenich as she left. Miss Jellenich glowered, even at Mike.

She was glowering more when Mr. Drake came in with a large box of pottery glaze but said he couldn't get clay until January. "But we were going to start our Southwest Indian art on Monday," sighed Miss Jellenich.

"Miss Jellenich," said Sean politely. He had been stuck more than once with the sink cleanup chore. "There's a big, heavy cardboard box under the sink marked *terra-cotta*. Isn't that a kind of clay?"

Miss Jellenich's delight over Sean's discovery soon faded. It was terra-cotta clay, all right. But it had sat on the shelf for at least ten years and was a single fifty-pound brick of solid rock.

"We could soak it over the weekend," she mused aloud. "But we'd never get it wedged enough, not even by Tuesday." Joe quit his desk art and sat up alertly.

Poor Miss Jellenich had other worries. There were those two yet-unscheduled conferences for Margie and Cheryl. And, instead of following her neat, one-at-a-time schedule, three of the mothers showed up together to confer right after the bell. Sean saw them waiting and might never have known why, except that he had had to come back for his reader.

Mrs. Radcliffe, Mrs. Yamota, and Mrs. Horwitz had compared notes. They were usually kind, soft-spoken, and friendly. But they seemed to be ganging up on Miss Jellenich, who looked more and more puzzled.

The mothers were loud enough to have to lower their voices when Sean came back in to get the book from his desk, but he could still hear them if he concentrated. He searched more patiently than necessary. And he concentrated.

"Even though Jerry is your best helper," said Mrs. Yamota, "he shouldn't always have to stay so late."

"I don't see how Rhonda can require so much tutoring," said Mrs. Radcliffe. "She's in the top reading group."

"Must the twins always stay to water the plants and straighten the shelves?" asked Mrs. Horwitz. "I don't even *see* all those plants!"

"But I *never* keep the children after school," protested Miss Jellenich. Now everyone was speaking loudly. "I'm clearing the way for a sabbatical to finish my master's degree, so I have to leave almost as soon as the children."

"Hmmm," said Mrs. Yamota. "Perhaps it's time to see Mr. Drake."

Walking very carefully on her high heels, Miss Jellenich followed the three fire-breathing mothers.

The next morning when the eight-thirty playground bell sounded, Sean dumped his books outside Room 6 because Margie and her father were inside looking solemnly at Miss Jellenich.

Sean didn't mention yesterday's eavesdropping to a soul, but he may have been the only child in Room 6 who knew why Margie's father disconnected his cable TV and made Margie bicycle down to the newspaper office to sign up for a paper route.

During the two conference weeks, Sean dawdled over getting to after-school football practice. The extra hour was a lot of time to fill, so he sat in the school patio for forty minutes each afternoon, doing his homework and watching parents come and go along the corridors. He hoped no one he knew would catch him taking Miss Jellenich's advice about good use of time.

Glancing up from his reading textbook, Sean was surprised to see a familiar gray dress. Cheryl Suzanne slipped out the doorway of the girls' room. When she saw him, she started to edge back in, then seemed to think it over. She squared her shoulders and walked over to sit on the bench across from him.

"Hullo," Sean said.

Cheryl swallowed. "Hello."

"It's nice to see your face. It's friendlier than your back."

"I'm glad you saw me. I wish you hadn't."

"Why am I X-rated lately?"

"Ooh, Sean, it's not *you*. Well, it *is* you. It's anything that's different. It con-tam-in-ates me!"

"You look unhappy. But not contaminated."

"That's 'cause you're the—the germ!"

"Thanks a lot!"

"My aunts say, 'Don't be different. Be exactly like us!' And the fifth-grade girls say, 'Don't be different. Be exactly like us!' I don't know what to do!"

"Miss Windemere sits on the North Pole and Margie's crowd sits on the South Pole?"

Cheryl chuckled in spite of herself. "And *you* just sit glued to the equator. But where," she asked forlornly, "do I sit?"

"On the lunch bench?"

"Silly!" With a giggly sniffle, she stood up. "I'm really disobedient. The worst I've ever been. I didn't give Aunt Laura the conference note. She doesn't want me hanging around any—uh—South Poles or any equators, so she brings the car to get me. She would confer if she knew about it—she's very law-abiding. But I just can't have her talk to Miss Jellenich. She'd find out how badly I get along with the rest of the fifth grade and might take me away. So I didn't tell her anything at all. After school, I hide out until the regular time, and she doesn't even know—"

Sean's glance fell on his watch. "Oh, you'd better hurry! It's past—"

"Indeed, it *is* past dismissal time," a voice said. "Young man, where is your mustache? Young woman, you have some explanations to make. And you will make them after I come back. I believe it is time I had a conference with your teacher! Wait in the car for me. *Alone!*"

Miss Windemere, majestic as a tidal wave, swept up the corridor to Room 6.

Overnight, the November air turned surprisingly cold, and next morning the children trudged to school against a brisk wind, securely wrapped in their second-best jackets and parkas. Their best wraps were still hanging in the Room 6 coat closet.

This morning, Miss Jellenich was in an unusually good mood. As the children hung or flung their wraps inside the coat closet, she commented on how neat and beautiful they all looked, especially their hair. Even Sean had told his folks about the nurse's visit with the Popsicle sticks.

Could Miss Jellenich's good humor mean that all her conferences were completed?

Miss Jellenich was downright cheerful when Joe asked if he could spend the day converting fifty pounds of solid brick into pottery clay.

"It isn't gray clay," he said regretfully. "But I like mixing stuff. I can work outside on a table." Three boys helped him drag the tub across the corridor to the strip of grass.

By recess time, Cheryl no longer sat by Sean. She had been moved to the seat next to Margie, thereby satisfying Margie's father and Cheryl's Aunt Laura. Neither girl looked a bit happy.

"The Endor girl needs socializing, poor child," Sean heard Miss Jellenich say to Mrs. Gresik as they met on yard duty. "I've put her with a girl who needs to tone down a little. They can give each other so much."

Sean just shook his head. Miss Jellenich had all the right reasons and all the wrong answers. Whatever Margie's dad and Miss Jellenich had talked over, nothing was going to tone Margie down. And Margie was certainly not the answer for Cheryl. She jabbered to the nearby children as if Cheryl weren't there. It must feel like being erased, thought Sean, for Cheryl didn't even poke her nose in the air anymore. And she stayed at a distance from the other children, including Sean. *Especially* from Sean, as if they hadn't talked yesterday like good friends.

As the school day warmed up, Joe had such a wonderful time creating red mud that he volunteered to stay to the regular hour, just to complete the job. All the other children, mostly in shirt sleeves, left at the bell. "Be sure to take your wraps with you!" called Miss Jellenich fruitlessly as they vanished.

When Sean popped in after school to get his forgotten windbreaker, he noticed a change. Joe must have helped Miss Jellenich move the portable coat closet. Sean guessed she had given up on trying to improve the class's memory or neatness. She just concealed the children's clothes. With a coat or a jacket on every hanger and hook, and with a dog bed of spare sweaters always spilling onto the classroom floor, the closet had been turned around like a high counter, facing the wall.

Conference time was over.

IX

Holidays and Strikeouts

On Thanksgiving Day, Sean's dad and Kelly baked a turkey while Sean and his mom and grandma watched the football game. As Sean ate with his family, he wondered if Cheryl Suzanne was enjoying a Thanksgiving feast. Did she just *think* turkey to have the meal ready and waiting the instant she opened her eyes?

Back at school, he didn't ask her. Sometimes, from across the room, her eyes wistfully met his, but at recess she still hid. There was never a good time when she was near enough to talk.

December came. The days were usually sunshiny. Almost every front yard had a bush of red poinsettias to remind everyone of the season. Last month's rains had brought new grass, a rich spring green. If Cheryl missed her white winter lawns of Massachusetts, thought Sean, she'd have to wait until August, when the sun bleached the Bermuda grass on most front lawns to white straw.

A few December days were icy cold and wet. The gray eucalyptus trees swayed, and the palms housed more tenants. Sean felt a little sorry for the visitors from Montana who had flown so far to escape the winter cold. In Room 6, the jackets and sweaters were recycled from the coat closet, which was moved out a little farther from the wall.

But everyone made a bargain with the TV weather forecasters: Keep New Year's Day sunny for the big parade and football game so that the rest of the world won't find out that loyal Californians sometimes fib about the weather.

Thanks to Joe, Miss Jellenich kept her own bargain. By the first week of December, all the empty ledges in Room 6 were covered with drying pottery, made while Miss Jellenich tried to inspire her students by reading aloud about Southwest Indian art and showing pictures. The children scooped and rolled and patted the clay in their own ways, paying no attention whatever to the examples.

Sean tried. He had rolled his rust-colored clay into the shape of a baseball to get it smooth. Next he shaped it like a slab of tomatoey pizza dough over a rounded rock. When it was firm enough, he added three knobby clay legs before lifting it free to dry.

Mike, with his mother's best rolling pin and twice as much clay as the others, made a rectangular slab box and lid.

Dino made the same kind of coil bowl he had made in kindergarten.

Joe made seven pink pinch pots shaped like trolls, then colored them with the grayest glaze he could find.

87

With a cookie cutter, Margie pressed out a slab of hearts. She poked a hole in each to hang it from a ribbon. She borrowed and ruined Sean's ballpoint pen to scratch *I LOVE YOU* on each one.

Cheryl, sitting by Margie, aimlessly punched her ball of clay. Seeing Miss Jellenich's glance, she perked up enough to flatten it out. It, too, grew into a heart shape. "You're copying Margie!" hissed Mike, and every head turned.

"Anybody can make a heart," said Sean softly. "No patent on that. On bumper stickers, hearts always mean love." He expected Miss Jellenich's chiding, but she just nodded and went back to the Southwest Indians.

Miffed, Cheryl wadded her clay back into a ball, then tugged off a small chunk and began to reshape it into a five-sided slab. "This doesn't mean *love*," she whispered to Sean, who had worked his chair closer. "It's a pentagram! My aunt took mine away."

This was the first time she had spoken to him in over two weeks. He felt a burden lift. "Does a pentagram mean—*hate*?"

"Not by itself. But it's a concentrator, a help-spell, to get what you really want."

"Make two of them," suggested Sean, thinking of baseball season and his nothing record from last year. "Maybe I can get out of right field and play infield next season."

He already knew what Cheryl wanted—to find a friend among the fifth-grade girls.

But she didn't say what he expected. With her voice

so low Sean could barely hear, she murmured, "They're so mean, I don't even want to like them or be like them. All *I* want is to get even."

"Southwest Indians," repeated Miss Jellenich dreamily.

The pottery emerged from the second trip to the kiln hard and glazed and gorgeous. Joe's raw gray glaze had changed with firing. Now seven bright-green trolls left him speechless. Cheryl's pentagrams looked mysterious.

The next art project was making wrapping paper. With pieces of cut potato, the children stamped tempera paint in the shapes of stars, candles, dreidels, and holly. Then they wrapped their pots, ready to go home for winter vacation. Sean planned to give his creation to his grandmother. After all, she had bought a lot of raffle tickets. Margie wrapped each of her hearts with special care. "I met these boys where I load up my papers on my paper route," she explained happily.

Cheryl wrapped only one of her two pentagrams.

In the last hour of the final school day in December, one committee served fruit punch, another put decorated bakery cookies on every table, a pizza delivery service brought five hot pizzas as a surprise from Sean's grandmother, and Mrs. Donlou came, just when everyone was cleaning up, to deliver the napkins Mike had forgotten.

Miss Jellenich gave everyone a comb and mirror case printed *GREETINGS FROM YOUR TEACHER*. All the girls were delighted. Miss Jellenich also had a pile of gifts from the kids, mostly bought from the lady who sold cosmetics and soap to the neighborhood.

Sean's present to Miss Jellenich was in an envelope that made it look like an ordinary greeting card until she opened it. Inside was a certificate good for one dessert at The Slinkery.

The last minute before Sean left for winter vacation, he felt a small package pressed into his hand. "To concentrate," whispered Cheryl, hurrying onward before he could speak. He knew from the shape, as dry tempera flaked off onto his fingers, just what was inside.

In eighty-degree warmth, the new year came. Then it rained all January. The children celebrated Martin Luther King Day with an assembly and a holiday, and looked forward to honoring Abraham Lincoln and George Washington in the same way. By February, Sean barely remembered last fall.

They never spoke, but once in a while Sean trailed Cheryl partway home. One day, he took the long way just to pass her house. He felt a twinge of sadness as three half-grown black cats raced across the lawn and through the picket fence to twine themselves about his legs. They barked happily at him.

Cheryl wasn't the only thing on Sean's mind. Baseball league tryouts were the first week of this month. With after-school practice daily, the teams met other tournament teams twice weekly throughout the spring. Any interested kid could belong to the league. The parents who started it had wanted to be fair. But, just as in school,

90

some kids rose to the top while others were hardly noticed.

It was easier, Sean felt, when your mom and dad had as much interest in baseball as you did. Mike's folks, for instance. From the time Mike was old enough to throw a ball, his folks had urged him along. And, sure enough, Mike's dad had been coaxed by the busier parents to be coach again this season.

Coach Donlou liked Sean, but he never called him an all-round athlete as he did Mike. A year ago Sean had sat a long time on the bench while Mike played first base every tournament game. How *could* you be all-round when you never got to show your goods?

Nobody complained that a good player like Mike got the breaks because he was the coach's son. Certainly not Sean's folks. They sometimes turned off baseball to watch public TV. They acted just as excited over Sean's art and music as over his sports. Whenever he told them his baseball troubles, they listened quietly. Then they soothed him by saying, "Isn't it a good thing you have other interests?" That was like saying, "Sorry you lost a dollar. Here's a penny."

In baseball, if you're good, you get better. If you're lousy, you don't get to touch the ball or bat very often. If you are in between, like Sean, you need a break to show your skill.

Sean knew it took a good fielder to make the team. A lot of kids on the bench envied him, but he had dreams of moving infield. At school, he usually played first base. Softball was not as big a deal as baseball, but at least he kept in practice. At phys ed time, Mike always chose to pitch. Miss Jellenich was impressed when he grandstanded. He reached out for easy balls, then rolled over and flipped with the ball in his grasp. So Mike usually pitched unless he traded off with Gayle or Margie on mixed-team days.

Miss Jellenich's conscience must have twinged now and then. "Mike," she would say, "why not play another spot today and give someone else a chance to pitch?" But then she would ruin it with something dumb: "Jeffrey, will you pitch instead?" Jeffrey stood with his mouth hanging open while the ball she tossed him landed a half yard away.

As a coach, Sean thought, Miss Jellenich was better at folk dancing.

The first day of mixed teams, Mike and Gayle took turns pitching. At bat, Cheryl hit an easy grounder to Mike. Cheryl knew even less about softball than Miss Jellenich did. She timidly started to run to first. Mike slammed the ball like a bullet to Sean with such unnecessary force that Sean bobbled it before he caught it, mostly with his chin.

"Sorry," said Sean, shaking his head to lessen the sting as Cheryl reached the base. "You tried." Cheryl smiled wanly and walked back to the lineup.

Mike, on the pitcher's mound, shook his head with exasperation and slapped his knee.

"Not so steamy," Sean called.

"Aw, you're holding the glove wrong," grumbled Mike.

Later, when Sean put Dino out at first, he tossed the

ball to third in hopes of tagging Joe. Joe stopped midway between bases and sprinted back to second and safety.

"What a dumb play!" yelled Mike. He never did that around Coach Donlou. "You should have seconded it! You could have put him out easy. Why don't you go back to kindergarten?"

After that, Mike pretended to be helpful. "Sean, you'll never get any distance if you hold the bat that way. Grip it lower!" The only time Sean listened, he struck out.

Mike pulled another mean trick. Jennifer was umpiring and Gayle pitched. Every time Sean was poised to hit the ball, Mike called his name. Sean either hit a foul or missed the pitch completely. When he resolved not to swing if Mike called, he missed good pitches and had a strike anyway.

"Boy," Mike needled him after Sean struck out, "you ought to go back to the babies. When are you going to learn to play ball?"

"If you'd lock your jaw, maybe I'd do better."

"Sean!" said Miss Jellenich.

"Sorehead!" Mike retorted, wearing a broad smile so that Miss Jellenich would fall for his friendly act. "Can't you take a little joke?"

In the third inning, Cheryl was safe on first. For a moment, she seemed to forget that she mustn't speak to Sean. As she watched her chance to run to second, she asked, "Do you like this funny game?"

"Sure," said Sean, a load lifting just to hear her talk. "It's better after school when I play with the guys. Except one guy."

"I know which," she said. "But at least the *rest* of the boys like you."

Then Rhonda hit the ball, and Cheryl sprinted to second. Sean was sorry he caught Rhonda's fly and automatically put them both out.

At league practice after school, things were not much better. Mike wouldn't be able to mouth off in front of his dad, but would Coach Donlou notice how much Sean had improved this year? Or would Sean be stuck in the outfield again? They ought to find out the starting team today. If Sean couldn't expect to play first base, maybe he could land an infield spot. But, after an hour, Coach Donlou was still holding off on a decision.

As Sean came to the park Saturday morning, he saw Margie, Gayle, and Rhonda gathered with other girls from Room 6. They'd had so much fun being pom-pom girls during the football season that they wanted to cheer the baseball team, too. They wore skating skirts.

Standing a short way off was Cheryl Suzanne Endor, watching the other girls solemnly. Sean bet her aunts didn't know where she was. "Hello, Cheryl," Rhonda said, but Margie nudged her and she did not invite Cheryl to join them.

Sean met the boys at the bench. In his new uniform, even Joe looked proud. He had four green smudges on his pants. "Grass stains," he said. "I like green now."

"Well, men," said Coach Donlou, "are you ready to show what you can do? Here's the temporary lineup."

When he read Sean's name for right field, Sean was

94

disappointed in spite of himself. It should have worked, darn it! He had Cheryl's pentagram in his pants pocket.

Right field was handy to the bleachers. Cheryl sat in the bottom row, near enough to talk. Would she? She watched Sean hunch and shift about, but the ball never came his way. "Do you like playing so far from the rest of the team?" she asked timidly.

"Sure, I like playing here in the boondocks," Sean told her through gritted teeth. "It took me half of last season to get this far." Dino, on the other practice team, slammed a high fly to left field. Sean grew alert, then returned to position.

"Not much happens where you play," noted Cheryl, relaxing like her old self. "Do you like it here because you can take it easy?"

"Well," grumbled Sean as he watched Joe hit a pop fly to Mike's waiting arms, "I could probably rest almost as much in a graveyard."

Cheryl's face lit up. "Then you really would like more action."

A low grounder skipped toward Sean. He reached for it and swung it to first, but not before George was safe. Mike mumbled something uncomplimentary, but Sean was too far away and Coach Donlou was too close.

"I wish I could pep things up," said Cheryl, "but I'm still on restrictions. My aunts are away today."

Mike grandstanded by stopping Greg's grounder and then overtaking and tagging George on his way to second. The fourth out was totally unnecessary, but great

95

for the spectators. Mike leered over his shoulder at Sean, and this time his voice carried perfectly. "See how a real pro does the job, Sean?"

"I really mustn't," Cheryl went on mumbling to herself. "Aunt Laura says I mustn't. She even found my clay pentagram in the wash. But *you* could help yourself."

Sean lost the last of her rambling mutters as he raced in to the backstop. When he came to bat, his practice team had two runs in and two outs, with Mike on third ready to be hit home.

Sean was a good batter. Mike wouldn't dare heckle him with his own dad looking on. So it wasn't Mike's fault that Sean messed up. It was just Sean's bad day. He fouled the ball four times, and then on the last swing popped a fly to third base.

Mike was left on third. Sean would be hearing about it all week. He walked to the field again, kicking the grass to work off his self-disgust.

Cheryl was still in the bleachers arguing with herself. "Aunt Laura doesn't know about games. Sometimes the rules need to be stretched." Then, louder, she said firmly, "Sean, put your pentagram inside your cap! I can't help unless you help, too."

Absently, with his eyes on the batter, Sean removed the pentagram from his pocket and stuck it inside the band of his cap. It was silly. It had to be silly.

But there was something reassuring in that slight pressure against his head.

The next hitter sent a liner neatly to Mike at first. In

the last instant, it wasn't so neat. It missed Mike's glove, ricocheted off the ground behind him, and bounced in a very unusual manner in little leaps to right field. Then, like a homing pigeon, it flew into Sean's glove.

Sean looked surprised and flung the ball back to the pitcher. With a runner on first, the game always got tighter. The next batter lofted the ball far over the players' heads to center field. It landed between center and right fields, and both fielders ran for it. A gust of wind turned it to Sean's reaching glove. Sean spun it back to Mike before the uncertain runner reached first.

Mike bobbled the ball.

Sean was disappointed at wasting such a nice throw. So, apparently, was Coach Donlou. He shouted something sharp at Mike. Sean felt a little uneasy, knowing a guy always wants to look good to his dad.

For the rest of the practice, Sean seemed to be in the hottest spot on the field. Every inning, his side came to bat following a remarkable and improbable double play out of right field. It just couldn't be happening. His teammates laughed and kidded him and enjoyed their good luck.

When they all gathered around Coach Donlou to rehash the game, Sean's hopes were high. Now he would learn if Coach planned to make any changes in the permanent team.

Even the girls crowded near. Margie started to yell, "Sean! Rah! Rah!" but the other girls shushed her.

"Here's the setup, men," said Coach Donlou. "I've been debating a few last-minute changes, but the list is

97

pretty much the way we worked it out the last few days."

He read off the names. Mike was still first baseman. Sean kept hoping to get second base or shortstop or even left field. He took off his cap and, lifting the pentagram carefully, brushed back his damp hair.

"Sean, you've certainly been handling yourself well. You've improved every game all year long. Mike, here," said Coach Donlou, looking down at his son with a frown, "runs too hot and cold." He held the scowl long enough for Mike to shrink a little. "But you always deliver what the team needs. Fact is, after watching what a handy man you are in right field, Sean, I've decided that that's where the team needs you most, Sean—right field. And that does it, men. See you Monday at practice and next Saturday in uniform for our first big game."

Sean hoped he hid his disappointment, but he saw it mirrored in Cheryl's face.

"I—I s'pose I should have minded Aunt Laura," she whispered as Sean passed. It sounded like an apology.

"Well," he told himself as he started home, "if I'm stuck in right field this whole season, I tell you what. I'm going to be the best right fielder this baseball league ever had!"

Much later, he remembered the pentagram. He might as well give it back to Cheryl Suzanne.

X

Tempers and Trouble

Every school day, Sean forgot to bring the pentagram to Cheryl.

Anyway, everyone was busy with school stuff. Visitors' Day was coming. Visitors' Day was not the least like the individual parent conferences. Everybody came at once, even neighbors and grandparents.

The classroom was so neat that Miss Jellenich had her social studies lesson out on the lawn to keep it that way.

She had lots of jobs for the kids. Sean got to cut out large paper letters for the bulletin boards. Miss Jellenich was suddenly worried about artwork to exhibit. The Southwest Indian pottery had gone home long ago.

Sean liked art. He couldn't draw as well as Jeffrey and certainly wasn't clever with clay, but he could build things. So, when Miss Jellenich said to bring in empty boxes to build a stabile construction, he brought in two full plastic grocery sacks.

"What's the junk for?" goaded Mike as he kicked one

bag under Sean's desk. Mike was still sore because his dad had chewed him out and praised Sean so much at practice.

Sean rescued his sack. He had large milk cartons and round ice-cream cartons. In his mind, he had it all planned. "I'm gonna make a castle," he mumbled. "It'll have pitched roofs and round corner towers."

At art time, Sean's table had more boxes than any other, and he had all the space he needed to work. "Perhaps some of you will share supplies with those who weren't able to bring any," said Miss Jellenich hopefully.

Weren't able—huh! Anybody could hit up the neighbors for the week's milk cartons, cereal boxes, or paper-towel centers. But Mike sat there with nothing but a puny half-pint milk carton he had fished out of the cafeteria trash barrel. Sean resented Miss Jellenich's suggestion. With just the right number of things for his castle, he didn't intend to share a one.

"Michael, will you take this note to the school secretary for me, please?" Miss Jellenich said.

"I'd be glad to," said Mike sweetly. "But I always get a chance to go on errands. Wouldn't it be less selfish to let someone else—maybe Sean—go this time?"

"That's very generous," said Miss Jellenich. "How about it, Sean?"

Generous—yecch! So that was how Mike was getting even for the game. Art time was fun, not like math. Sean was so angry, he simply couldn't speak. With his face flushing, he stood up and reached for the note. Miss

100

Jellenich smiled and busied herself straightening the back cupboard.

The school secretary was busy on the phone, so it took ten minutes for Sean to get back to Room 6. Miss Jellenich was still happily moving stuff around the cupboard shelves.

Sean hurried to his table. Where were all his boxes and cartons? The only things left were an empty oatmeal cylinder and a flat box that had once held his dad's birthday necktie.

Sean closed his eyes and clenched his fists and counted to fifty before he was calm enough to look over at Mike's table. Sure enough, Mike was making a magnificent castle. He had already cut windows in the milk cartons and stapled the cartons tightly to the ice-cream containers.

Sean walked directly over to Mike's desk and glared. If they'd been outside, he'd have beaten Mike to pieces. "You took my boxes," he said, gritting his teeth and clenching his fists.

"Oh, yes. Thank you," said Mike with a broad, cheery smile. "I did take a few."

A small voice inside, his dad's voice, seemed to be warning Sean. "Speak up for your rights. You may have to let it go if it hurts only you. But don't give anybody room to hurt you twice." This was the worst thing Mike had ever done.

"I need them," Sean said, getting a little louder. Miss Jellenich turned to look. "All of them. *Those are my boxes.*"

"Oh?" Mike was all innocence. "I thought you meant to share them. Didn't you hear Miss Jellenich ask? And then you were gone so long, and naturally I helped myself to one or two. Too bad you won't be able to use these now, but here's one you can have. I'm not using it. Take it." He handed the half-pint carton to Sean.

Sean set it down like it was poison and turned his back. Mike just wasn't worth it. He was such a little-kid bad sport.

"I tried to be nice," said Mike plaintively.

Sean sank into his chair. He breathed so heavily for a minute that the children around him were very silent. Miss Jellenich looked troubled. She *had* to know Mike was wrong, even if she'd been too busy to watch. "I'm sorry, Sean. I *did* urge the children to share."

Gradually Sean's anger let up. "Okay, Dad," he said in his mind. "No point in upsetting Miss Jellenich. Mike didn't hurt anybody but me. And I'll never give him room to hurt me twice." He looked listlessly at his desk. What kind of stabile could he make with one round oatmeal carton and a flat, rectangular box? He looked around for inspiration.

At her table with Margie, Cheryl pensively turned a shoe box over and over. Sean hoped he'd see a gleam of mischief in her eye, but his spirits fell at her usual solemnity. As he watched, she cut away the sides of her box, leaving the corners for legs. Now it was a table.

Well, he had to get started on his own job. He took the lid off the necktie box and held it crosswise against the bottom to make an X. With a brad fastener, he punched through both sections at the middle of the X. Then he made another hole high on the side of the oatmeal box. He spread the prongs and stood his creation—a scrawny windmill—on its base.

He glanced over to check on Cheryl. She had cut two crude silhouettes from her unused box lid. Now she fitted them to one side of the table, like children side by side in a classroom. Sean suddenly recognized them—a fluttery Margie and a huddled, withdrawn Cheryl. She finished pasting and sat back with a stony expression. Sean felt a lump in his throat.

"What an inventive idea!" Miss Jellenich told Sean. But she oohed and ahhed over Mike's castle.

The next day, the children painted their stabiles. The paint was mixed with glue to stick to the shiny surfaces of the boxes. Joe stirred up a cup of green tempera and painted a green village of upside-down yogurt cartons.

Sean finished his whole project in fifteen minutes. He yawned and pulled out his reading book.

Mike tried to catch his attention. Sean tried not to notice while Mike painted away, concealing the lettering *GRADE A MILK*. Across the back of the milk carton where Miss Jellenich wouldn't see it, Mike painted a bright-red message: *SEAN IS A DOPE*. Then he tapped Sean on the shoulder to read it. Sean closed his book with a snap.

"Sean," said Miss Jellenich as she looked at the clock. "If you are through with your work, help with the sink cleanup."

Mike returned virtuously to his painting.

As the children finished one by one, Sean cleaned their brushes. He knew how to shape the bristles for the next user. He was still seething when Mike finished, just before the recess bell rang. Mike carried the red paint jar over to Sean.

"Ooops, sorry!" said Mike. He probably just wanted to scare Sean by pretending to spill the paint. But Mike pretended too well. "You tripped me!" he accused unfairly.

Sean hadn't tripped anybody. But Miss Jellenich looked up to see the wall behind the sink spattered with gluey red paint. "Oh, Sean," she moaned. "Can't you do anything right lately? And tomorrow is Visitors' Day. Well, you'll just have to do your best to clean up so your parents will see a neat room. Class dismissed."

While Sean stayed in all recess to remove paint and glue, the other boys played two innings of softball. Mike hit a home run. He told Sean all about it when the class returned, while Sean had another little private conversation. "I think I gave him room again, Dad."

Mike's desk was near the sink, where he could "accidentally" trip people on their way to get a drink. From behind his social studies book, he bragged. "It was a great hit. I could have crawled the bases and still got home on time."

Sean went on wiping the sink.

"Too bad you didn't get to watch. Might have helped your game."

Sean wished the spot he was scrubbing was Mike's face.

"Don't act so sore," whispered Mike huffily. "I'm trying to help you be a good ball player."

"Yeah. You're a great help," muttered Sean, dropping the last wad of paper towels into the basket.

"Sean," said Miss Jellenich. "Come to your seat."

The class grew unusually quiet again as Sean sat down. Miss Jellenich looked tired. The main bulletin board was still unfinished. She sorted through the stack of letters Sean had cut out so carefully and then searched the classroom for someone who had finished the day's work. Then she sighed and seemed to make up her mind.

"Michael," she said in a low voice, just loud enough so every child in the room looked up. "Michael, will you put these letters up along the bulletin board here? Then, if you have time, you can choose some good examples of the art projects to place on the table in front of it."

Sean kept his face expressionless. Mike always got the good jobs, but for once it had seemed that Sean could have been chosen. He had worked hard on those letters. Miss Jellenich had talked as if he could do the whole job. Now, because of Mike's messiness, Sean had been left out.

Sean's cheeks grew hotter than before. He opened his book, but he didn't read. He just stared as though the marks on the page had grown meaningless. Once in a while, he glanced up to see what Mike was doing.

Mike pinned up the letters:

WELCOME PARENTS!

Then, farther down the wall on the second bulletin board, he placed the words:

THIS WORK IS FUN!

It wasn't bad, but, of course, it wasn't what Sean had planned. He forgot himself and watched openly as Mike selected the best art projects for the display.

Best, huh! Mike lifted his own red castle and set it in the place of honor at the center. Then, with a great deal of exaggerated pondering, he selected three more—Gayle's and Margie's and Jeffrey's.

Miss Jellenich's mood improved. She asked the children to put their books away. Then they had to clean their desks inside and out, getting rid of any stray papers or candy wrappers or penciled scribbles. Everyone was to make the room neater for tomorrow.

Some children asked to do special little jobs like straightening the bookcases or putting the encyclopedia volumes in order. Except for the C encyclopedia. It had been missing since they studied Columbus.

"Sean, will you please—" she began, and he sat up straighter, hoping for a chance to do something a bit special, "uh, empty the wastebaskets?"

"No," said Sean, under his breath.

But he did it.

XI

An Unusual Visitors' Day

From the very first minute, Visitors' Day was special. The room surely looked different. Long before the first bell rang, Sean saw Miss Jellenich was in the classroom arranging bookcases and tables in unnatural neatness. The children, who arrived early to put away lunch boxes and get balls for games, were so impressed that they stayed inside to help.

Joe, who had filled a wastebasket with wads of green paper when he cleaned his desk yesterday, found more— enough to half fill another.

After the bell, the children stood for flag salute without wasting time. The parents were due in fifteen minutes. The children were nearly as nervous as Miss Jellenich. Margie was struck silent. Steve and Dino didn't punch each other. Mike even wore a necktie.

The tables had been moved to form an empty square at the front of the room. Extra chairs for parents lined the sides and back. The children were supposed to be busy reading when the parents began to come in, but their eyes didn't move from the pages they started on. They kept their heads down, but they sneaked sideways glances.

At the front of the room, Miss Jellenich began to speak nervously in her stagey voice. The children could look up now. "We are glad so many of you came," she said. And there were a lot! The children squirmed and looked around the sea of grown-up faces. Sean's mom and dad were sitting near the door. So was Sean's grandmother, who looked a little like Miss Jellenich, gone fat. Mike's mother and father sat nearby. Sean glanced quickly over the faces to see if Miss Windemere had come. She was nowhere to be seen. He was relieved for Cheryl, but a little sorry for her, too. Then he thought of the clay pentagram he had remembered to bring at last.

Miss Jellenich was still talking. "First, the children want to show you one of the dances they have learned. Will those children who are to demonstrate our square dancing please form your set?"

Sean went reluctantly to the empty space at the front of the room, but he cleverly slid the clay pentagram into Cheryl's hand when he passed. Six other children followed him and formed a set. "Oh dear," said Miss Jellenich. "Ruth is absent. Let's see—Cheryl Suzanne, will you take her place as Sean's partner?"

The reason Sean had been selected to dance was not so much that he was a good dancer but that he was a bad speller. When Miss Jellenich had held tryouts for the spelling bee, Sean had been among the first to sit down.

He didn't mind terribly about missing spelling or having to dance. He had decided to be polite and not act as if the girls were poison, the way Dino and Steve did. It was okay to dance with Cheryl Suzanne. His missing partner, Ruth, was one of the lumpiest girls in the room. He preferred girls skinny and straight. Like Cheryl.

Cheryl looked about as if to check whether her aunt had come. Her expression of anxiety faded. Then she glanced at Sean with a mischievous grin.

It was a good thing Sean had practiced. From the minute the record started, he had to let his hands and feet take over. His mind grew all aboggle at what was happening to his square.

The voice on the record called, "Swing your partner." Sean and Cheryl Suzanne danced a buzz step, right feet touching, left feet sliding.

The caller said, "Swing your corner." Sean danced a buzz step with—Cheryl Suzanne?

The voice on the record said, "Allemande left." Sean stretched his left hand to—Cheryl Suzanne!

The voice on the record said, "Grand right and left," and every single girl in the chain seemed to be Cheryl Suzanne! She was the girl in front, the girl behind, the girl across.

When the record spun to a finish, Sean's knees were too weak to lead Cheryl back to her chair. She led him. "Thank you," he said, as they had been taught. "All of you."

The parents all clapped politely. They had not seen anything wrong. Miss Jellenich came back up in front.

"One of the features the children have planned for you today is an old-fashioned spelling bee." Sean couldn't remember ever having planned it. Miss Jellenich had just told them they would have it, and they did.

Jeffrey, who could spell much better than he could pitch a softball, was absent. Sean wondered who would take his place. As the six children lined up at the front of the room, he saw Miss Jellenich look worriedly over the group. Her eyes swept over Sean in a hurry. Finally they settled on Wendy.

"Because one of our contestants isn't here today, we'll ask another fifth grader to fill in." Cheryl Suzanne gave a soft, little cough, and Miss Jellenich looked her way. "Sean, will you take Jeffrey's place, please?"

Miss Jellenich looked just as shocked as Sean, but neither could back out now. Sean walked slowly to join the rest. He saw his dad's raised eyebrows and his mother's incredulous, pleased smile. Why, she was just as proud as if Sean had *earned* this honor. But his grandma— who had saved every one of Sean's thank-you letters— looked happily horrified.

Sean glanced past the stunned Miss Jellenich to Cheryl Suzanne. *She* looked very cheerful.

Most of Sean's friends watched in sympathy. His sick feeling grew at the expression on Mrs. Donlou's face. *She* looked so proud, you'd think Mike was about to be inaugurated as president of the United States.

Sean knew who had caused this. Why had he ever given the pentagram back to her? But Cheryl's face now held only encouragement. He felt in his pocket. There,

110

bumping around with his latchkey and three quarters, was the distinct five-sided shape of her clay pentagram, back with him once more.

Miss Jellenich explained that she was giving hard words, straight from the sixth-grade book. Mike was first. He spelled *separate* with no trouble.

Gayle spelled *exercise*. At Sean's turn, Miss Jellenich's voice faltered. He could see she wanted to give him a word like *cat*. "*Unwelcome*," she said, and closed her eyes prayerfully.

"*Unwelcome*," repeated Sean. "*Unwelcome*."

"Yes," said Miss Jellenich softly. "*Unwelcome*."

"Will you use it in a sentence, please?" asked Sean, to gain time.

Miss Jellenich came up with a schoolteacherish sentence. "Polite children are always welcome, but impolite children are unwelcome."

Sean's vision blurred. He wrinkled his forehead and twisted his mouth and squeezed the pentagram. Then, to his surprise, he seemed to see the last two letters from one bulletin board move over to the beginning word of the second bulletin board. The letters lined themselves neatly in front of the words already there.

As plain as day, he could read the word *UNWELCOME* just behind the parents' heads.

"*U-N-W-E-L-C-O-M-E*," he spelled easily. Miss Jellenich let out her breath with a long sigh. The boys and girls all sighed, too.

Sally and Gordon went down on the first round. Miss Jellenich found some harder words. "*Rectangular*," she

111

said at Sean's next turn. He looked at the bulletin board, but no word awaited him there. He looked at Cheryl Suzanne as he squeezed the pentagram. He could see the letters suddenly form right inside his head.

Sean's mother was glowing with pride as if she were being coached by Mrs. Donlou. Sean hardly dared to catch her eye. Mike spelled *candidate* and Sean spelled *equally*. Three more children went down.

At last, only Sean and Mike were left. Mike wasn't looking quite so pleased with himself. Sean felt totally in a fog, almost too bewildered to care.

Mike's next word was *ghostliness*. He licked his lips and attacked it slowly. His mother hunched forward to watch each letter form. "Why, Mike *has* to win!" Sean thought to himself. "He has to win at everything! His mother and father can't face letting him lose."

Sean looked across at his own parents. They had taken the morning off from their jobs just to watch him do a dumb folk dance. He wasn't the greatest student or the best athlete, but he was their son, Sean. He didn't need to be a superson. He could just be himself. But Mike— poor Mike—was *nobody* unless he won.

Sean's word was *witchery*. He repeated it, looking from Mrs. Donlou's tense face to his own mother's calm smile. She was herself again, and there was love in her eyes. He looked at Dad's "Okay, boy" grin. And Grandma actually winked.

Then he looked at Cheryl Suzanne and ever so slightly shook his head. She looked surprised and somehow pleased. He pulled his hand out of his pocket. No word formed in his head.

"*Witchery*. Uh, *W-H-I-C-H-E-R-R-Y!*"

Miss Jellenich shook her head absently, looking relieved. "*Witchery*," she repeated for Mike, who spelled it without a flaw.

The parents all clapped for Mike. Sean palmed the pentagram and slipped it to Cheryl on the way back to his seat.

Happy and flustered, Miss Jellenich next told the parents about the children's work. She mentioned all of their lessons. Finally she said, "And, of course, the children have time for self-expression. You will notice the bulletin board on the side wall and the samples of their work over here."

All eyes swept left and then right, and some of the parents turned backward to see the bulletin boards. A gasp arose from the crowd. Sure enough, the signs now read:

UNWELCOME PARENTS!

THIS WORK IS F!

Sean exchanged a look with Cheryl Suzanne, who held a cupped hand for him to see the pentagram.

As all eyes were riveted on Mike's beautiful, red castle, a gust of wind seemed to push it. It began to fall apart. Staples spurted outward. In slow motion, the red towers toppled. The large milk carton with the hidden message,

SEAN IS A DOPE, fell over on its side, and some of the paint chipped as it fell. Now, partly in Mike's paint and partly in the original printing, it read clearly: *SEAN IS GRADE A!*

The last pieces of the castle fell across the table where Mike had crowded together all the stabiles he had judged too poor to display. A piece hit Sean's windmill and knocked it sideways, spinning the arms. As one last guest entered Room 6, the wind blew across the windmill blades and made them spin more quickly. Then, while the parents watched in stunned amazement, the windmill slowly lifted and floated over their heads, moving for all the world like a hovering helicopter. No one spoke. Everyone in the room held his breath.

Slowly, slowly, the helicopter floated across the room and then, just as if it had a mind of its own, crash-landed on Mike's head.

Mr. Burgess dashed over. "Don't break it! Don't break it! I'm in aerodynamics—I want to see that model!" Ignoring Mike, who was rubbing his bump in more bewilderment than pain, Mr. Burgess looked over the dented windmill. He turned it on all sides. He spun the blades. They scraped and stopped. He dropped it. It simply dropped. "Most amazing," he said. "Most amazing."

Somehow, Miss Jellenich got the rest of Visitors' Day over with, but nobody seemed to care. Mr. Burgess left cradling the windmill and repeating, "Remarkable. Remarkable."

But Sean was worried. He had seen Cheryl's face the

instant after the helicopter landed on Mike. She was looking through the doorway.

There stood Miss Windemere, gray and grim and frowning. A real witch would know that the strange happenings could not have taken place without help.

Or could they?

As Sean went over to say hi to his mother and father and grandma, something inside kept worrying him. Cheryl Suzanne stood looking up at her aunt as if she had been the most disobedient child in the whole world. Miss Windemere's eyes were like icicles.

What would happen to Cheryl now?

XII

Waiting and Worrying

His concern about Cheryl Suzanne didn't stop Sean from enjoying his favorite time of the year. Spring, which had tried so hard to come in December, now really burst out in March. The ugly, gray ground cover called ice plant reddened. In another month, every parkway would be a blaze of magenta. The homely Indian hawthorn hedges foamed with pendants of pink.

From his three bedroom windows, Sean could see the knife-edged blue ocean to the west, snowcapped Mount Wilson to the east, and the new-leafed elm tree to the north. He drank it all in each morning as he hopped from bed. Three months from now he might see nothing but a curtain of smog.

But right now, he had no troubles at all, except Cheryl Suzanne Endor.

For two long weeks, Cheryl had not come to school. Was she sick or was she in deep trouble?

With any other friend, Sean would have just picked

up the phone. Or he would have walked over to her house and pushed the doorbell. But with Cheryl, how could he? Wasn't he, himself, the main reason she'd been grounded? He couldn't even walk slowly past her house after baseball practice without getting her in deeper trouble.

When Sean did stride briskly along on the opposite side of the street, he barely looked sideways for fear Miss Windemere was watching. But he could see the leggy kittens tumbling on the lawn. One leaped to the fence rail and yapped at him.

He was always busy with sports and homework. But sometimes, when he let himself into the empty house after his workout, the loneliness reminded him of Cheryl. He had Mom and Dad and Kelly coming to join him soon, but she just had those sullen old aunts in her big, drafty prison, and no one could be lonelier than that.

Kelly was home for a few minutes today before dashing to work. She seemed to sense that Sean was restless. "How is Cheryl Suzanne Endor these days?"

"I just don't know," muttered Sean.

"Oh?"

"Well, I finally tried to call her. Actually, I tried three times. They have an answering service." He tried to repeat what he had heard.

" 'The householder has gone for a spell,' the tape said. 'At the sound, leave your name, coven, and message.' I waited for the tone. It sounded like clanking chains. Then, as soon as I gave my name, the phone went dead.

117

"And the next time I tried, the tone was like bones rattling. The tape heard my voice and shut me off after three words.

"And the last time I called, I thought I heard Cheryl in the background when the tone came. It was like a raspy hinge. And then a voice said, 'Go away,' before I even cleared my throat. The Windemere telephone doesn't like me."

Sean found himself telling Kelly more about Cheryl. Kelly could tune right in on feelings. She seemed to know about hurting inside yourself for the pain inside someone else.

"Cheryl has tried to live by her aunts' rules in a world that doesn't match the childhood they had," Kelly said. "Think of the changes in the world since her aunts were small! Cheryl is a single child, but her aunts came from a large family and had one another to turn to. Cheryl has nobody her own age. I'd guess her aunts don't realize how much she really needs friends."

"They're mean," said Sean.

"You mean they're strict."

"Okay, strict. So strict it feels mean."

"Since Cheryl is very talented, they don't want her to waste her gifts by being an ordinary person."

"*I* like being ordinary."

"What if Mozart or Bach had decided to be ordinary?"

Sean remembered a few boring piano lessons. He held his tongue.

Kelly outguessed him. "Suppose the members of the

118

Baseball Hall of Fame hadn't used their talents, even if they could get more friends that way?"

"Okay, okay. I guess one of the things I *like* about Cheryl is that she *is* a witch. I'm just sorry she's not a happy witch."

Kelly craned her neck toward her handbag. "Toss me my purse. Thanks. Sean, try to understand the aunts. They want Cheryl to learn skills her ancestors kept hidden for hundreds of years. They're afraid of outsiders, even though they don't need to be. I bet they'd have a great time if they invited a few Cal Tech professors to join their coven. But they really aren't *bad*. They would never hurt anyone. Why, Cheryl said they grow melons without water that take only a month to ripen. They want to send seeds to desert tribes to fight world hunger. And Cheryl helps with the spells. Isn't that worth a friend or two?"

"Yes," said Sean. "No." He frowned. "I don't know."

Kelly fished for her car keys. As she reached the door, she turned back and gave Sean a tight hug. "Cheryl is lucky she has *one* friend!"

Mom and Dad were both home tonight. Sean's spirits lifted. After dinner, he went upstairs to do his homework. It went so quickly he almost felt he had the ceramic pentagram back to help him concentrate on the reading work. In a puzzling way, he felt as if something gently controlled him. As if something watched.

"Lights out in half an hour," said Mom, coming in for

her good-night kiss. "Have I told you today how proud you make me?"

"Twice," said Sean. "Once more won't hurt."

"I'm proud of you and I love you. And you need a haircut again."

"You only say that because you're still bigger'n me."

"Bigger'n who?" Dad was at the door to say his good-night.

"When it comes to haircuts, I'm bigger than both of you," said Mom.

"We better do something about it," said Dad, "or she'll cut off our allowance."

Sean and his father shook hands solemnly. "I think I'll get my hair cut next month," Dad said.

"September for me," said Sean. They hugged all around. When the door closed after them, Sean meant to brush his teeth and dress for bed. But he felt drawn to the window.

"It's about time," said Cheryl Suzanne. There, waiting in the tree as if she had been there since Halloween, Cheryl signaled impatiently for Sean to come near.

The limb looked pretty far from the sill, twice the distance he could reach. Even Dino, with his long arms, couldn't reach that branch. "Grab my hand," Cheryl said, stretching out. Sean didn't hesitate. He held on to the sill and touched her fingers easily! She clasped his hand lightly. He boosted himself forward, and his toe settled into the tree crotch as he swooshed to Cheryl's side.

"Hello. I missed you. Why are you here?"

"Equinoctial coven. But my birthday is nearly here,

120

and I had to see you once more. They can't watch me every minute."

Birthday? Sean was more puzzled than ever.

Cheryl climbed down like a cat in spite of her long, black skirt. Sean took longer, fishing in the dark for toeholds, but it was not at all hard, not like the daytime. He stood beside Cheryl in his yard. His family was still downstairs. Where could they talk?

"Come on," Cheryl said.

"Where?"

"To the coven, of course. I have to help some, but not all the time. I can sneak you in, and we can talk while my aunts are busy with the meeting. It may be our last chance. Hurry. We've got to get there before the wizard comes."

Sean blinked the daze from his mind. A fat, full moon had risen, but he felt almost invisible as they jogged down Diablo Drive and up to Cheryl's corner.

XIII

Stowaway
in the Coven

"Shhh," cautioned Cheryl Suzanne as they approached her three-story house. The tall, narrow building was bathed in moonlight. Each shutter and dormer window stood out brilliantly. "It's always bright on party nights," Cheryl said. "We always celebrate esbath on the full moon, but aren't we lucky to have a full moon this equinox, too?"

Avoiding the bright front steps, they slipped into the side yard. Cheryl led the way around to the back door.

"There you are, Cheryl Suzanne," called a brisk voice. "Do wash your hands and face and come help serve the guests." Then the voice spoke to someone in the room beyond. "I do wish I knew what is keeping Judith. She is always here to greet the wizard, Darien."

"In here," whispered Cheryl. She thrust Sean into a broom closet. He knew it was a broom closet because it held a dozen brooms. He sat on a stool, puzzled at what to do. The lanky, black kittens immediately came to him. One jumped on his lap and growled.

Cheryl came back in a minute. "I have to serve tea

and cakes—herbal tea and oatmeal cakes, flavored with rosemary and rue. I'll have to wash dishes after, too. But the rest of the time, they won't want me at the coven. They never do on esbath or equinox, because I'm not eleven yet. We'll just hide on the staircase and peek down on them and hear what they decide to do with me."

On tiptoe, they climbed the back stairs and walked through a gloomy, gray hall to the front stairs. "Here. Hunker down so they can't see you. This is where I watch."

Sean settled himself between two banister posts.

Five women, all in long black dresses just like Cheryl Suzanne's, sat below. Beside each woman was a man, also robed in black. The men wore small caps like black ice-cream cones on top of their balding heads. They were all in a circle, except for Miss Windemere, who paced back and forth.

"That's my Aunt Laura," whispered Cheryl. "Those are my other aunts on the chairs. That's Aunt Margaret, and there's Aunt Becky and Aunt Carol and Aunt Patty."

"Our six warlocks are here, and we await Darien, the wizard," said Cheryl's Aunt Laura, Miss Windemere. Sean studied her face, sharp-nosed and lean. "Tonight is important. It is necessary that we be represented by six witches as well. As you can see, Cousin Judith has been delayed. I told her last time that poor-quality straw would give her too many transportation problems.

"Speaking of transportation, one of the topics we must discuss tonight is transporting our melon and squash seeds to have-not nations. Spells aren't as useful nowadays. Credit cards and cash are sometimes handier. Ah, well, with Judith delayed, I have another plan. We must proceed, using our niece, Cheryl Suzanne."

Cheryl's hand gripped Sean tightly on his shoulder. Her expression was one of stark amazement. "They can't mean it. I'm not ready! I thought this last time they'd leave me alone."

"You're dressed for witching," said Sean. "You *look* ready."

"I know. But they're deciding about *me*! I'll have to go down. Don't make a sound." She walked slowly down the stairs.

"How old is Witch Cheryl?" asked one of the warlocks.

"A goodly ten, Warlock Dennis," said Miss Windemere. "Not yet eleven. She has not qualified as a full witch yet, but she can raise the power. She is not very good with a broom yet, even for sweeping, but she is proficient in some spells without help-spells. I have had to caution her against spells used just to amuse, but she is nearly eligible for full status. It will be our decision tonight when to grant it and where to send her."

"Then let us enter her on trial tonight, or we cannot proceed with our equinoctial coven." The witches and warlocks all nodded their agreement.

A quavery doorbell tinged. Sean looked the same direction as the others. "It's Darien!" everyone said in a hushed voice. "It's our wizard." They all rose to face the door.

In came a very solemn man. He wore a black robe to his heels, and he tossed back a small hood to reveal thin, white hair. He carried a large book. Sean squinted to read the title—*Book of Shadows*.

When the wizard took his seat, the others did likewise, except Miss Windemere and Cheryl. Miss Windemere led the girl to face the wizard. "This is Probationary Witch Cheryl Suzanne who, unworthy as she is, will make our group the traditional thirteen."

Cheryl did not look at Sean, but he *read* her apology inside his head. She was going to be stuck here longer than just to serve tea and cakes. She couldn't get back to him the rest of the evening.

"Has she been cleansed?" asked Wizard Darien.

"Yes. She washed her face and hands up to the elbows in salt water," explained Miss Windemere.

"It itches," acknowledged Cheryl.

"Silence," said Miss Windemere.

Miss Windemere now wheeled a tea cart past the rim of black-garbed worshippers to the center of the circle. It did not contain food or drink, just a candle, an odd-shaped cup, and a strange metal thing. "The sacred objects—the candle, the chalice, and the censer—are here," said Wizard Darien. The *Book of Shadows* was placed among the objects.

"The meeting may now begin," said the wizard. "Let us hear the minutes of the last meeting."

Cheryl's Aunt Becky read a short report on the Candlemas festival of February 1: Thirteen members had attended. Witch Margaret read correspondence from the chapters in Salem, Massachusetts and Galveston, Texas. Dues of silver fifty-cent pieces were to have been collected, but because of the shortage of silver coins, a live lizard was accepted from each member. The sacred wine had been drunk.

"Corrections or additions?" asked the wizard.

"This isn't quite a correction, but we will have tea tonight," said Miss Windemere. "This is a temperate house, and we have a minor child among us."

Sean was startled, thinking he'd been discovered, and then realized she meant Cheryl Suzanne. He had barely relaxed when he heard something whir past his shoulder. An owl flew in and sat on the tea cart, blinking at the candlelight. No one in the circle showed much interest.

"In deference to our youngest member's bedtime," said the wizard, looking over his spectacles at Cheryl, "we will have our reading from the *Book of Shadows* at nine thirty instead of midnight."

"Time isn't as important as it used to be," sighed Miss Windemere. "Daylight saving time and digital watches made us an hour wrong at the Lammas meeting, too."

The wizard opened the book and read a long passage in a foreign tongue. Cheryl yawned. The cats came in from the kitchen, and she patted one absently.

"And now," said the wizard, "to call the power. If this little group is in perfect accord tonight, there is much we can do. Quickly, let us summon the power and then on to the decision about our probationary witch."

Now the only lights in the room were moonlight from the window and the one small candle. The thirteen members joined hands and stood with heads turned upward, eyes closed. All eyes but Cheryl's. She looked at Sean, and her face was worried.

"Do you feel it?" asked the wizard anxiously. "It seems very slow coming forth. What foreign spirit is holding it back?"

Cheryl's eyes grew wider and wider. Her mouth formed an unspoken *"No-o-o-o!"*

Sean heard a stir on the staircase. Three black cats were racing up to him.

"The spirit is fighting to break through. Why won't the power come?" questioned the wizard. The others mumbled and grumbled.

The cats had been friendly before, so Sean stretched out a cautious hand.

"Woof!" they barked. "Woof! Woof!"

All eyes flew open and looked toward the staircase.

"A stranger! A male stranger!" called the wizard. "Come down, sir."

"It's the same boy from All Hallows' Eve and the outdoor lunch benches," pronounced Miss Windemere. "Why are you here? Come down at once!"

Penitently, Sean walked all the way down the long staircase, cats barking at his heels. He looked helplessly at Cheryl, hoping she wouldn't have to suffer for this. "Uh—would you like to buy some raffle tickets to help our baseball fund—?"

"Baseball! *Baseball!* A waste of time, with people starving in this world. Cheryl Suzanne has been raised for important work, not for frivolity." She stared at Sean with eyes like green ice cubes. "Just go. You won't be able to tell a soul about this." Miss Windemere pointed to the front door.

Sean stopped in midstride and squared his shoulders. He turned back to face them. "I was wrong, I guess, to come where people don't want other kids. But you're wrong, too. Kids need some fun. They can't always be perfect and never make mistakes."

Thirteen people were staring at him, all aghast. And Cheryl's face was the whitest of all.

Sean tried hard. "It's not Cheryl's fault, honestly. I just hung around and bugged her. She tried to keep me from talking to her. It's really my fault."

"No, it's not!" said Cheryl, suddenly as noisy as the barking kittens. "It's not Sean's fault. He's my *friend*! I never had a friend before. That's why I broke the rules. And I'm not sorry!"

Sean stood helplessly as he watched Cheryl's appalled family circling her.

He felt totally ignored. He edged to the door. As he stumbled out, Sean heard Miss Windemere say, a little sadly, "Cheryl Suzanne Endor—you, young lady, are hardly deserving of the honor of being a witch!"

He didn't run, yet Sean seemed to get home much more quickly than the two had come. He knew his mom and dad were still downstairs in the living room. He was ready to go in and face the music, but Miss Windemere was right. He couldn't bring his hand to turn the front doorknob or to ring the bell. "You won't be able to tell a soul about this," she had said. She was also making sure he wouldn't lie.

His feet seemed to pull him along to the side of the house and the big elm tree. It stretched very tall above him. He began to climb.

When he reached the limb just opposite his window, there was no way to get across. It was just too far away.

"Reach!" he heard a voice in his mind say, a girl's voice. "Reach!"

It was a long way to fall, and he tried not to look. He reached across, farther and farther, and then dropped.

Sean caught the sill effortlessly and swung a leg up and over. For a long moment, he sat there panting. Then, not even bothering to undress, heartsick at Cheryl's future, he fell across the bed.

XIV

April Foolishness

On April first, Cheryl Suzanne came back to Room 6. Sean was so glad to see her that he ran down the sidewalk to intercept her at the school-yard gate.

But she might as well have been her answering service. "I can't talk," she said.

Sean felt a surge of disappointment. But it was not as strong as his relief that she was back at last.

Did she realize what day it was? Her special talents were made to order for April Fools' Day. But Sean was so glad to have her back in school that he didn't even care that the day went its usual way.

Dino offered everybody a package of cardboard strips cut carefully to fit inside the spearmint wrappers that once contained chewing gum. Mike kept sticking dumb *KICK ME* notices on people's backs. Actually, Sean would have put signs on backs, too, but he could never have gotten away with it. Everyone in the class knew his unusual spelling.

Once the class was seated, Sean felt someone lightly pressing something against his own back. He guessed immediately who had put it there, from the words *PINCH ME* on blotchy green paper. "Well," whispered Joe defensively, "I forgot to celebrate Saint Patrick's Day."

As Mike rambled around the long way to go to the pencil sharpener, Sean felt another small pressure. He twisted like a gymnast to read the message upside down:

CHERYL ♡ SEAN

He couldn't get even because Mike didn't seem to be around part of recess time. But, when Miss Jellenich unlocked the self-locking door to let them back inside, both she and the class stood amazed at the backward message written across the chalkboard. With a smile playing about her mouth, she read it slowly to herself, but the children had to borrow Margie's hand mirror to read it.

Miss Jellenich quit smiling when she tried to erase the board. Someone had slipped chalk inside the felt strips of the eraser, and every stroke made a bigger scribble than it erased.

Joe spent the noon recess showing everyone a dead, green finger inside a matchbox. "I forgot to bring this on Halloween," he apologized, as the girls all screamed and then looked again. Nobody near Joe ate much lunch.

Mr. Drake made Joe throw his empty matchbox with the hole in the bottom into the trash. Joe wore a green middle finger the rest of the day.

As they left the cafeteria, Sean cornered Cheryl. "Aren't you going to play one little trick? Just one?"

"No, and I told you I can't say one word to you. I wouldn't be back to school at all if that police officer hadn't come to see Aunt Laura. He said I have to go to school to learn unless someone at home is cer-ti-fied to teach. Besides, she's still angry with you for talking the way you did at the coven. And at me, because I stood up for you."

For somebody who couldn't say one word, Cheryl was pretty talky. "I'm sorry, Cheryl," said Sean earnestly. "I guess I was disrespectful. I just knew it meant a lot to you to be with other kids. It's not your fault that you have—talents."

Margie walked by with Rhonda and looked right past Cheryl. But this time, Rhonda slowed just a little. She wore a tentative, shy smile, as if a word from Cheryl might make a difference. Did Cheryl sense a change? Sean wondered. But Cheryl just moved her head to stare at the beams over the corridor. Then, timidly, half doubtfully, she looked back at Rhonda. Sean saw a ghost of a smile flick over her face, too.

After lunch, Miss Jellenich had to confiscate Dino's fake gum because somebody put a real wad of gum on the floor where she stepped. Then she had to ask the custodian to turn off the room's drinking fountain because it was partly plugged with clay and the water squirted sideways all over her.

When Miss Jellenich finally got back to her desk and found the plastic cockroach Steve had slipped into her grade book, April Fools' Day was over by ultimatum.

"Oral reports tomorrow," growled Miss Jellenich.

"April fool?" the children asked hopefully.

"No. Genuine reports. You can't have forgotten, with three full weeks to prepare."

Just before dismissal, Mr. Drake came to the classroom door. Everyone was messing around instead of getting oral reports ready for tomorrow. Miss Jellenich sat dreamily at her desk, water-splashed, her hair out of place, and a smudge of chalk on her nose. "Your sabbatical was okayed," Mr. Drake said, a little loudly to be heard above the noise.

"April fool?" she asked doubtfully.

"Absolute superintendent truth."

"What's a sabbatical?" asked Cheryl.

"Heaven," said Miss Jellenich. "Sheer heaven. Class dismissed."

The next day Sean was as ready as he'd ever be to recite what he had learned about North Dakota. He had practiced on Kelly to gain confidence, but he still dreaded social studies time. After all, North Dakota was kinda nowhere compared with Alaska or Hawaii. The books he'd looked at didn't give it any Oscars. His written report, looking a little tired, had at least a skillion misspelled words.

He was glad Miss Jellenich called on him early. Sometimes she worked from the bottom of the alphabet upward on her grade sheet. *Wilkerson* came just above *Yamota*. Bad as his talk was, Sean got it over fast.

Just before Mike spoke, Cheryl Suzanne reported quietly on Massachusetts, a lucky choice because she'd missed several weeks of school. When Mike made a yawning noise in the middle of her talk, Cheryl's eyes flashed fire. Sean had a feeling the pentagram might get a workout.

When Mike's turn came, the class quit doodling and showed a stir of interest. Mike never got the shakes in front of an audience. He carried his thick booklet to show

134

some of the logos and maps his computer supplied. Most of his notes were on small sheets of paper.

"My report is sixty-six pages long," he smirked. "I used our word processor to write it. And I have Polaroid pictures from my trip there last summer."

Cheryl's pencil rolled off her desk, and she bent to pick it up. Mike pointedly waited for her. "Now that I have everybody's attention," he said, almost duplicating Miss Jellenich at her crabbiest, "I would like to tell you about the state of Hawaii."

Sean's sidelong glance at Cheryl cheered him enormously. She was breathing deeply, shoulders back, lips firmly together. Then the wind came.

Only two windows were open but Mike was in a terrific draft. His notes kept fluttering. A gust lifted them, and they slid from his fingers. They whisked out of reach as he flailed and grabbed. One card fluttered over onto Miss Jellenich's desk. She reached for it, then glanced more closely and turned it over.

From several seats away, it was easy to read:

It was one of the April Fools' Day notes Mike was sticking on backs the day before. The corners of Miss Jellenich's mouth fought to stay down. "Well, that's interesting, Mike. But what does it have to do with Hawaii?"

Mike finished telling about Hawaii, but his notes were mixed up, and so was he.

"B-plus," thought Sean, with deep satisfaction.

After Cheryl Suzanne had played a joke, she seemed easier to talk to. When school was out, she even waited for Sean to walk with her.

"Aunt Laura isn't coming for me today. All my aunts need the car to go to Madrona Marsh to find where the birds are planning to migrate. They'll drive from there to Marina Del Rey to visit the lagoon stopovers."

Sean tried to picture all of Cheryl's aunts in that little, black sedan. Even for witches, it must be uncomfortable. "What's their reason?"

"They're trying to find carriers to take melon and squash seeds on a flyway into the desert lands of Africa. Aunt Laura grumbles about the California life-style. Even the birds don't like to give it up."

Sean changed the subject. "My birthday is a week from Saturday," he said. "I'll be eleven. Are you eleven yet?"

"Next month. I still get to be ten for a while."

"Get to be? Don't you like becoming a year older?"

"I'd rather stay ten a long, long time. Ten hasn't been much fun, but eleven is a whole lot worse. It's so hard."

"Hard? For you?" Sean was astonished. "I thought

136

you could do about anything. And when you're eleven, you'll be a full-fledged witch, and you can do a lot more."

"Not everything. I already do a lot of things easily, but that doesn't get me what I want. The things I do well don't make me any friends, except you. Maybe grown-up witches don't care, but I do."

Sean was nearing his turnoff, but he dawdled. He listened as Cheryl went on confiding.

"I know how to make the wind blow Mike's notes, but that doesn't get other people to like me. Look at Mike himself. He's been angry with me ever since I came, even before I played a single trick on him."

"Don't tell me you'd like Mike for a friend!"

Cheryl went right on. "I find some things easy, all right, while I watch *you* work very hard. But *your* work pays off. Everybody likes you."

"Huh! Not old Mike. Not Miss Jellenich."

"Well Mike's a special case. But you're all mixed up about Miss Jellenich. She trusts you. She gives the real responsibilities to you. She knows who she can depend on."

Sean's mouth hung open as he absorbed this.

"And, as for Mike, have you ever noticed how he looks at you as if he wants to be more like you?"

"*Me?*"

"Mike envies you. In a way, he's sort of like me. He has no real friends. *You* have dozens. His folks won't accept any failures, and he pushes people around so he can always win. But name even one friend Mike has."

"He *is* kind of a loner," mused Sean.

"There's another way Mike and I are alike," said Cheryl.

137

"Some things are *too* easy for us. Our folks think every-thing is easy, and they expect a lot of us." Her face grew bleaker. "I'm going to hate being eleven!"

Cheryl studied the sidewalk a long time. " 'Bye," she said suddenly, spinning about. She ran, not up her street but back to the corner, bunchy dress billowing, toward the shops and stores in town.

Nothing made much sense to Sean, but he thought a lot about what Cheryl had said, especially about Mike. At practice later, he watched Mike thoughtfully. When Mike taunted, Sean looked for reasons, and the taunts didn't irk him so much.

Sean watched Mike's dad, too. Even when Mike made a hot double play, Coach Donlou was dissatisfied. "Don't home it! Go for the force-out. Try to get the runner. The name of the game is *win!*" And Mike slumped, just a little.

Cheryl was right.

XV

Out in the Outfield

For the rest of the month, spring vacation and baseball filled Sean's days. Eight weeks into the season, Sean had grown adjusted to right field. The play was lively enough to keep him hopping. Maybe next year he'd be ready for an infield spot.

He could feel his own daily improvement. His muscles minded him better. Each catch was more exact, each throw more direct, each turn at bat more powerful.

His tournament team was doing well. In nine games, they had won six. They had a good chance to top the district.

On Sean's eleventh birthday, his team won by four runs, a fine birthday present. But the same day, there came a blow.

Their best pitcher's dad was transferred to a new job in central California. The family would move away in one more week. The boy who had pitched most heavy innings all year was a real specialist, but he'd just played his last game.

Coach Donlou had the rough job of finding a reliable pitcher for the rest of the season. Sean, glued forever to the outfield, let the coach worry it out by himself. Grandma was waiting at home with a big birthday dinner, with nothing canned or frozen *or* nutritious. Sean spent the rest of Saturday being properly spoiled and stuffed.

After dinner, the whole family went to the boutique. "It's your birthday, Sean. You can choose anything in the store!" said his mother.

Sean looked obediently at the lacy aprons and satin pillows and stuffed teddy bears, waiting until Mom sent Dad to the storeroom to bring out his real present.

"We were going to give you this on your thirtieth birthday," apologized Dad, "but after Visitors' Day, we figured we'd better not wait."

It was his own home computer, mostly for games. "But there's a gadget for correcting spelling on your stories and reports," said Dad. "It won't cure you, but it will patch and plaster the worst spots."

Sean played three games while Mom and Kelly showed Grandma the new things in the boutique.

"See our ceramic good-luck charms," said his mother. "These were Kelly's suggestion. The samples are going well, and we've got the exclusive."

Grandma admired everything and finally bought a tile printed *NO PEDDLERS OR AGENTS* at the special one-hundred-percent discount Mom offered family members.

The following week Coach Donlou called a special

Friday practice before Saturday's game. All week, he had tried Steve and Dino, both pretty fair relief pitchers, at the mound. Today, sounding very cross with Mike, he asked him to try pitching. Mike was pretty good, Sean thought. But not good enough to suit his dad. If Mike got it over the plate, it was slow or high or just predictable.

Sean watched and worried right along with them. They took a break while father and son talked it over. "It doesn't mean anything to me," thought Sean, as he glanced idly over to the edge of the field.

Margie and Gayle and Rhonda were in their skating skirts, ready to lead the cheers. But a familiar-looking girl in an unfamiliar outfit came hesitantly around the corner of the bleachers. It was Cheryl Suzanne Endor, wearing not a bunchy, gray dress, but an ordinary knit top and jeans! What would Miss Windemere say if she knew?

Sean tossed the baseball from one hand to the other and watched as the cheerleaders noticed Cheryl approaching. They appeared to check her up and down. Then Sean saw Margie shrug and jerk her head for them to turn away.

But the dark-haired girl didn't turn. As if making a decision, Rhonda kept facing Cheryl. Sean could almost read her thoughts by her expression, although he was too far away to hear what she said as she turned back to Margie, or what Margie snapped back.

Then Rhonda, in her bouncy skating skirt, stepped

away from the other cheerleaders and walked straight toward Cheryl Suzanne. She said something. Cheryl, her back tense and straight, suddenly relaxed.

Together, the two girls climbed to the highest seats in the bleachers. When they saw Sean looking at them, they both waved.

Hey, things were really going better for Cheryl! When they had parted on the sidewalk ten days ago, he'd been her only friend. Now she had Rhonda, too. He felt happy for her, but—maybe—a teeny bit let down. In some ways, it had been very special to be Cheryl's only friend.

The feeling faded as Sean felt his own confidence surging up inside. Things would go better for him, too. Maybe he wasn't glued to the outfield forever.

"What do you think, Sean?"

"Me? Oh, I think Mike will make a great pitcher. He's got a good eye and throw."

The team guffawed. "I'm asking you if you'll try your hand on the mound," said Coach Donlou patiently.

"Oh. I'm sorry I didn't pay attention." This was Sean's big chance!

His heart began to beat fast. "N-n-no," he said.

Where was that new confidence now? Coach Donlou and all the team were staring at him. How could he explain?

He drew a breath and plunged in. "I don't think I'm your guy. I've had a lot of practice on long throws and I can do base work pretty well. But I really don't have the short plays down cold like Mike or Steve. And I—I just can't pitch more than half an inning in a whole

142

game. I lose control after a dozen windups. I just don't have the endurance to pitch the long haul." He looked around at the quiet team. "Thanks, but—well, I'm not ready yet."

Mike's jaw had dropped. Sean, feeling both sad and happy inside, looked past Mike to where Cheryl Suzanne watched with Rhonda. Had Cheryl made him say that? It was the truth. Now he'd messed up the biggest chance he'd had this year. He tried to feel anxious about it, but he couldn't. He felt fine.

Coach Donlou's face cleared. "You may be right, Sean." He pondered. "But what about first base? We'll need Steve and Mike to catch and pitch."

Mike, who was seldom at a loss for words, suddenly began to stammer. "At school—in softball, that is—Sean plays first base. Don't let him sell himself short. He's really good at first." Mike paused, looked surprised at himself, and then looked pleased.

"Hmmm. Men," called Coach Donlou, "let's work around this combination. We'll keep Steve as catcher, put Mike as pitcher, and give Sean first base. Let's give it a whirl!"

They clicked!

The three boys seemed to be one machine. Catching, pitching, first base—wow! The practice team came to bat against them, but the ball control was all on the side of the three. From the first throw-around, they just knew they had *it*.

"We'll try it this way in the game tomorrow, with Dino as relief pitcher," said Coach Donlou.

He looked as proud and happy as Sean had ever seen him. And it wasn't for Mike alone. "I'm telling you now, boys, it looks pretty permanent. We've got a snap in our teamwork we didn't have before!"

XVI

The End of the Witch?

Sean caught up with Cheryl as she waved good-bye to Rhonda at her corner. "Wait up," he said.

Cheryl turned. "Sure."

"I guess—I think I ought to thank you. But I wish you hadn't helped me this time."

She had been half dancing, enjoying the fit of her knit shirt and pants. But now she grew serious. "Today is my birthday. I should be eleven."

"Oh. Happy birthday." They just stood there. She looked at him expectantly. But the light didn't dawn.

"You don't see, do you?" He shook his head. "I *should* be eleven. But I wasn't sure myself about training to be a—a person with special powers." It was a little as if she couldn't even say the word *witch*.

He waited.

"All people with special powers have to go through special training. Up until their eleventh birthdays, they stay on probation. Like teachers. Like Miss Jellenich.

Teachers have to get ready a long time before they can teach."

"So?"

"Remember April second? Remember the oral reports, and afterward you walked me partway home? Well, I ran down to The Slinkery."

"You saw Kelly? She never said. But she keeps a secret when I ask her to. No reason she wouldn't treat you the same. I told you she really understands people."

"Well, I was nervous and I kept playing with the pentagram, and she made me sit at the window table again. While I waited for her break, I argued and argued with myself, but I knew from the start that the only way for me is to be what I am and to do what I have to do. But I kept thinking, 'Wouldn't it be neat to wait awhile to be a full witch?' Why must it get all serious, just because I become a year older?

"Then Kelly sat with me. I don't really remember what I said or much of what she said, except that I should go to Aunt Laura and really talk things out. Then Kelly noticed the pentagram."

By now Sean was thoroughly puzzled. "Well?"

"She liked it. She said she knew your mother would love to sell some like it in her boutique as good-luck charms and that maybe other shops would like them, too. 'Mom receives parcels for her business from all over the world,' Kelly said. 'She can save shipping costs by buying stuff made right here.' Then I just went home."

"I still don't see—"

"Well, I *did* talk my problems over with Aunt Laura.

146

I expected her to be angry, especially when she saw the pentagram. She said I'd made it all wrong and that it would never make decent spells the way it was messed up. She said I must be getting very good at spells using only subvocal formulae to have helped you in the spelling bee and to have messed up Mike's speech. She said the clay pentagram was hardly good at all for witchery. But Aunt Laura is an animal conservationist. She liked the idea of selling pentagrams to replace rabbits' feet as good-luck charms."

Sean blinked.

"Selling the pentagrams can give our coven some legitimate income, Aunt Laura says. She wants to ship our melon and squash seeds to Africa right away. She tried enlisting the migrating birds for carriers, but birds need swampy rest stops, and oases are too few. None of the birds follow flyways across the desert lands where the hungriest people live.

"I told Aunt Laura what Kelly said about your mother getting packages through parcel service from all over the world. Our pentagram sales could pay for mailing costs to send seeds where the birds can't even fly."

Sean stood still and whistled his approval.

Cheryl went on. "And then Aunt Laura told me that on the night of equinox, you and I had made her do some thinking. Yesterday while I was practicing my formulae and spells with chants and gestures, she called my other aunts to watch. They all agreed that, even when I don't say the words out loud, I can call the power very well."

"Like an A student," said Sean.

147

"A-plus!" said Cheryl. "Then Aunt Margaret said to Aunt Laura, 'Why can't we ease off on Cheryl Suzanne's lessons for a while? She's studied so hard here in California that it would be a pity to send her away for advanced training before she's had a chance to enjoy living here. Why, the poor child has never even been to Disneyland!' "

"You didn't tell her—"

"Even witch children have *some* sense!" said Cheryl, shaking her head. "Then Aunt Patty reminded them about my birthday. Of course, that stopped them cold, because when apprentices turn eleven, they have to get serious about witchery. I felt so terrible I just burst out and said, 'I wish that witches could take a sabbatical!'

"That's when Aunt Laura wrinkled her forehead and snapped her fingers for her owl to sit on her shoulder. He helps her think. 'Esbath—sabbath—Roodmas— sabbath—Lammas—sabbath— Why, witches *invented* sabbaticals! There *is* a sabbatical from witchcraft! I'll get in touch with the Master Coven immediately.'

" 'Mistress Coven,' corrected Aunt Becky. She's a feminist.

"So Aunt Laura contacted the witch headquarters— it's easier these days by satellite phone than by spells— and you know what?"

"Tell me," urged Sean.

"Well, witches can arrange for sabbaticals just like teachers. It's a time of rest from witching. And Aunt Laura applied for a year's sabbatical for *me* starting yesterday, before my birthday. I don't have to be eleven for a whole

148

year. I don't have to practice witchery unless I want to. There may be penalties if I slip. And Aunt Laura still insists I must be inconspicuous. But I told her the school clothes she picked for me attract more attention than knit tops and pants, and she came around. At school, I get to dress like the other girls. But you know something—?"

Sean opened his mouth, but Cheryl didn't give him time to say a word. "Today Rhonda didn't even notice what I wore at all!"

"Well, *I* did," said Sean.

"Oh, *you*," said Cheryl, dismissing him as if boys didn't count. Then, seeing his expression, she flashed him a happy smile. "You. Sean Wilkerson. The best friend of all. My being left out didn't bother Rhonda, but it did bother you, and you've been a friend anyway. You taught me I can be what I have to be. Thanks to the sabbatical, though, I can wait awhile to do what I have to do."

Sean was thinking. "All this change happened *yesterday*? Then, the game today—you didn't help—?"

"How *could* I?"

"Then getting to be first baseman, that was—?"

"Whatever help you got came from believing in yourself."

And Cheryl Suzanne Endor skipped on down to the friendly, tall, old house where three full-grown black cats meowed around her feet, for all the world like ordinary pets.

All the last week of school, Sean felt a glow of happiness. Summer was coming, and fifth grade would soon

149

be gone forever. Even social studies wouldn't be around for nearly three whole months.

Mr. Drake spread the leftover wraps from every coat closet all over the patio lunch tables. Sean waited until the mob of mothers had claimed all the outgrown garments that they could identify. Then he found his own missing windbreaker and a sweater he thought he'd lost back in fourth grade. The chewing gum in the pocket nearly broke his teeth.

Because Sean had had such a good year in Room 6, he decided to bring Miss Jellenich a big, red apple to celebrate the last day.

Big, red apples were hard to find in June, but that didn't stop him from doing something nice, especially since he could have been one of the reasons Miss Jellenich was going on sabbatical.

With Joe proudly helping him carry it on the last hazy, blue day of school, Sean brought Miss Jellenich a big, green watermelon.

Saying good-bye to all his fifth-grade friends took so much time that Sean was almost the last student to leave Room 6. He looked about at the vacant coat closet, the bare bulletin boards, and the strangely empty tables. As he left the room, Miss Jellenich surprised him with her warm smile and an almost-hug. Sean hugged her back. If any kids saw him, they'd forget by September.

Outside, the day was turning bluer. Mr. Drake stepped through his office doorway to call, "Have a good summer, Sean!" Sean waved.

Halfway up the block, Rhonda and Cheryl lagged along,

heads together. Sean could have hurried to join them but he had a feeling that, right now, he wasn't needed. He watched them and thought again of Cheryl's words a few days back.

"*I don't have to practice witching unless I want to. . . .*" Would she ever want to?

"*There may be penalties if I slip. . . .*" Would she dare?

"*I must be inconspicuous. . . .*" How could mischievous Cheryl Suzanne Endor hide her ability to cast spells?

Sean shook his head. Well, he'd be there if she ever needed him. Meanwhile, she was in good hands with Rhonda Radcliffe.

He chuckled to himself. Wow, was Rhonda due for a big surprise! Penalties or not, *of course Cheryl would slip!* It was going to be a great summer.